"To be able to say how much you love is to love but little."

Petrarch

© Kate Fitzroy 2018

Fresh and Fruity

Wine Dark Mystery: Case 10
Verdicchio, Italy

by

Kate Fitzroy

PROLOGUE

'Go on... tell me how much you love me, Eve.'
'Don't be ridiculous, Adam. I've told you a million times already and its time to get up now.'

'Oh, go on, it's such a good game, and we haven't played it for ages. I'll give you a starter question then. Do you love me more than...more than that bracelet, I bought you in Frascati?'

'That's even more ridiculous. How can I compare how I love you with how much I love a bracelet?' I twisted my hand in the air so that the silver chain of vine leaves twisted in a shaft of morning sunlight. 'It is quite perfect though. Anyway, I could ask the same... do you love that old leather thong bracelet that I gave you more than you love me?'

'OK, I agree, it is a stupid comparison but don't you dare dis my bracelet. I've never taken it off since you gave it to me. I was mighty impressed, by the way, Bulgari and all.'

'You're so girly, Adam. You do so love your designer brand names, don't you?'

'Girly? How can you say that after last night... and this morning? I'll show you how not-girly I am.'

'Oh no, you won't. We have a ten a.m. meeting with Melanie Powers. I must get up and shower right now.'

'Why don't you then?'

It was a good question and one I couldn't answer as I looked into Adam's sky blue eyes. It was very difficult saying no, or rather no, not again, not now, to a man who looked like Jesus. His long, dark blonde hair was tickling my bare shoulder as he stretched across me. No beard or moustache but, apart from that, he was so Christ Superstar or maybe a Botticelli? My thoughts drifted away as he moved over me.

1

'And I suppose you'd like the same driver on the trip?' Melanie Powers, my agent, was peering over her black-rimmed glasses at me and then to Adam as she spoke. Her surname, Powers suited her very well. It was Dickensian in its aptness. Powers, yes, she certainly held powers of persuasive coercion. It was difficult to stand against any decision she might make on my behalf. Fortunately, I hardly ever needed to disagree. From the moment we had met, she had orchestrated my career as a wine writer and continued to create my success. So, I was grateful to her and her considerable powers and tried to ignore the fact she was so obviously besotted with my new husband, Adam Wright. Now, as she still looked at him, waiting for my response, I was amused to see how he calmly withstood her fierce stare. Was he aware of the effect he had on her? Well, on most women, in fact, and not to rule out some men, children and any number of animals that I had seen him tame. But, he was mine. I knew it with all my heart and so easily dismissed any stupid jealousies that came our way. He had a natural charisma, it floated around him like a magic cloak. Then, Melanie returned her attention to me, sighing as she continued,

'I suppose I know the answer. You'd both like me to ask Bernard Guillaume if he is free to chauffeur you around Italy again?'

'Would you, Melanie?' Finally, I spoke, attempting to sound as grateful as I felt, 'We hate to ask him now that he is married and living in the south of France. But maybe if you asked...' I let my voice tail off, and Adam spoke up,

'Could you, Melanie?'

Now I saw Melanie begin to melt under the strength of his sky blue-eyed gaze. I almost felt sorry for Melanie, how could she resist such a simple, heartfelt request? I thought back, just for a brief moment to earlier that morning when I had succumbed to him. Our love-making had almost made us late for this meeting. I sighed and gently massaged the small of my back, feeling the sweet ache of tired muscles.   Then, with a sigh that echoed mine, Melanie smiled. How her face changed as she relaxed. The hard line of her bright lip-sticked mouth softened, and she spoke quietly, maybe with resignation,

'I know, I know... you both rely on Bernard. Well, he has been on all your other assignments, so I see no reason not to ask him again. The production company of your up-coming follow-up TV series will fund any of your whims, Eve, you know that.'

'Thanks, Melanie, all due to you. I should never have dreamed anyone would want me for a TV programme.'

Adam sat forward and laughed,

'Isn't my sweet wife always so modest, Mel? You know, when I was on assignment as a war photographer in Afghanistan, she was the top female fave among the boys. Every Saturday, either at the base camp on widescreen or on someone's phone or laptop in a tent, there'd be a scramble to watch her programme. Four and a half hours time difference but it made no difference to the boys.'

'Honestly, Adam, I can hardly believe that,' I frowned at him, 'How many soldiers would be interested in a programme with me roaming around some vineyard in France or Italy?'

Adam laughed again, 'I didn't say they were interested in wine.' Then he looked at Melanie, 'Modesty again, Eve doesn't realise she is sexier that Nigella in her Greta Garbo trench coat. The shrug, the frowning eyebrows... I mean, look at her now.'

Now Melanie laughed and even relaxed her rigid shoulders under her dark grey suit jacket.

'You know, Adam, that's exactly it. Eve is completely un-self-aware. It's a winner on the screen.'

I continued to rub my back as they carried on discussing my talents between them, almost as if I weren't there in the room. I looked out of the long plate glass window behind Melanie and wondered, idly, how she could turn her back on such a view. The City of London stretched out, grey and misty damp, the solid dome of St Paul's nestling amongst the forest of high rise offices. The glass was splattered with fine rain, and I longed for some southern sunshine. To stretch out and feel some warmth on my skin. How would it be, September in the Verdicchio region, the verdant Le Marche? The heat of August would have died, but we would probably land into mid or high twenty degrees. I felt a surge of energy at the thought and returned to the conversation that had continued without me.

'... she knows her onions though, or rather grapes.' Adam was still talking about me to Melanie. I interrupted,

'I am here, you know.'

'You mean, you're back with us.' Adam stretched out his long arm and ruffled my hair. 'I know you, Eve Sinclair, you looked out the window and went into one of your reveries.' He nodded at Melanie, almost conspiratorially, 'She's always doing that... I call them Eve-reveries.'

Melanie laughed, and I decided it was time to pull rank. I sat up straight and smoothed my hair back behind my ears as I said,

'Never mind all this chatter. I have another meeting in half an hour. So, if you'll contact Bernard and let us know, Melanie, as soon as possible. I'd like to get away by the end of this week. If Bernard is agreeable, then Adam and I will fly to Ancona or Bologna and meet him at the airport.' I stood up and held out my hand to signal the meeting was over.

Outside in the light rain, Adam opened up his ancient black umbrella, and we stood close together under it for a moment.

'You don't really have another meeting, do you, Princess?' Adam looked down at me and then kissed the top of my head.

'Don't call me, Princess.' My response was automatic as I said it every time.

'I know, I know, you think it's vulgar. But when you behave in your Princess mode, I can't resist. I just love the way you wrapped up that meeting. So sexy when you snap into command. Quite the budding dominatrix.'

I gave Adam a sharp dig in the ribs with my elbow, but he didn't seem to notice. He was, as usual, enveloped in his old Parka and well insulated. I turned up the collar on my Burberry trench coat, pushed my hands deep into the pockets and shivered.

'You're cold and hungry, let's get brunch in that ever-so-trendy caff over there, the one with all the dark glass and steel. In the meantime, have a butterscotch.' Adam pulled out a silver foil-wrapped sweet from the endless supply he kept in one of his many pockets. He unwrapped the large sweet, and I opened my mouth for him to pop it in as he said, 'There, a little sugar is what you need. Now you won't be able to argue with your mouth full. God, how I love your mouth.'

Quickly, he stepped back a pace and, with the lightning speed of the professional photographer, he took my photo. I glared at him and, of course, he took another. Then, I began to laugh, and he clicked again. I grabbed his arm as we made our way across the square toward a dark-windowed café.

Adam pushed his camera back in his pocket and lowered the umbrella over us as he kissed me,

'Sure you wouldn't rather go home? I could make you one of those pancakes you like, and then I could massage your back.'

He knew everything about me.

2

Adam was very busy at the kitchen end of our open-plan loft apartment. He was whistling and trying to look accomplished as he knew I was watching from where I sat on the sofa. Celebrity photographer he certainly was but celebrity cook he most definitely was not. I had tried not to laugh when I saw him throw the third pancake in the bin. Not that I could cook anything at all. My childhood and life before marriage had not prepared me for housework or cooking. I was almost the typical spoilt child of divorced parents, brought up by a succession of nannies, tutors and then serving time in an uncivilised but horribly expensive public school. Even my time up at Cambridge had been a privileged life of eating in halls or the best restaurants. I like food and, of course, I love good wine. But then, very suddenly, I was no longer a typical spoilt young woman. My wealthy life had vanished when my father had fallen from grace in the money world of the City. Not only had my wealth disappeared but my father had vanished. His tower block had shattered into bankruptcy and reclaim. Only Bernard, the chauffeur who had driven me around for as long as I could remember had remained. Loyal, kind, sternly silent at times, he had been my salvation. Now, three years later, I knew that my father had disappeared into a Buddhist retreat in India to lick his wounds. But had he thought about me? Had my mother cared or even bothered to leave her latest husband to come over from California? No, suddenly I was totally unsupported.

My family homes, yes, homes in the plural... the Kensington townhouse, our manor in Sussex and estate in Scotland... all claimed to offset my father's debts. When my Coutts Silk card had been refused, I began to panic. I had retreated to my farmhouse in Provence which was fortunately in my own name, a twenty-first birthday gift from my father. I hid away, living on the funds from the sale of my jewellery and cars. I was content to sit under an olive tree and write my poetry, read my books on medieval history, dip into the turquoise water of my little swimming pool and be cared for by a kind couple from the local village. To anyone who hadn't known my past, I was still living a privileged life. But, and it was a small word of vast threatening darkness, but... I knew it couldn't last. My emergency fund would evaporate into the maintenance of the farmhouse and wages for my cook, cleaner and gardener. I had lived a sheltered life, but even I could work that out.

My PhD in medieval literature wasn't much help unless, perhaps, I could teach? I had only considered that option for a micro-second, knowing how useless I would be at that particular profession. Then, I remembered that I had qualified as a Master of Wine while up at Cambridge. I'd had very few friends there but had been included in a dangerous group of students who met to taste wines. In this strange, esoteric little club, I had been surprisingly popular, well, not so surprising as I was the one who could afford the most expensive wines of the world. I had undertaken the learning of oenology in the same devoted and earnest way that I applied to my literature studies and finally been awarded the prestigious Masters qualification. Would it now, in my newly impoverished state, be of any use?

My father had been a close friend of the editor of a renowned Sunday paper, and I decided to telephone him from my Provencal refuge, anxious that he would just berate my father or simply not take the call. I had been relieved and surprised to find that he thought my father wrongly accused of corruption. He was a large, kindly man, and I had known him since I was a child. We chatted for a good while and soon I had wheedled my way into writing a weekly wine article in his Sunday colour supplement. Then, I had met Melanie, and she had taken me over. My shyness was her challenge. I smiled as I thought back to the first days of my recovery from certain poverty. I was still shy but becoming used to this new exposed life as a TV celebrity. Melanie forced me to appear on panel games and dreadful quiz shows. So, my life had somersaulted into new and independent ways.

But nothing had prepared me for meeting Adam Wright. Melanie had persuaded him to accompany me as the photographer for a prestigious book on wine. A glossy slab of a book that was destined to grace the coffee tables and bookshelves of the wealthy. Adam had not long returned from the war fields of Afghanistan, and his work had won awards and was exhibited in galleries across the world. Why had he accepted this assignment? Perhaps he was in recovery from shock and wanted a pleasant and straightforward job touring the vineyards of France and Italy? Maybe it was the powers of Melanie? At first, I had found it hard to adapt to his easy-going East London manner and speech. Very soon I had realised that my own recent distress was nothing compared to what he had witnessed and emotionally reported. Adam had strode vigorously into my new-made life bringing a sharp blast of reality... and then, love.

My thoughts were abruptly interrupted by a crash from the kitchen followed by a muttered curse and then silence.

I looked across to the kitchen end and saw Adam was turning up the extractor fan to high. There was a slight aroma of burning over the better smell of coffee brewing.

'How about toast?' Adam looked back at me and smiled. Oh, that slightly crooked smile that made my heart melt down into my boots or somewhere low in my body.

'Lovely. Can I have honey on it?' I called back, stretching.

'You can have honey anywhere you want, my love.' Adam strolled toward me, his light blue eyes softening into a darker blue. I knew that intense look well. I stretched again, rubbing my back, 'You promised me a massage, didn't you?'

'So I did, so I did. How about you go to bed, and I'll bring you some toast and coffee?'

'How about we have toast and coffee later?'

'Well, I guess that could be arranged. I'm suddenly not so hungry for food.'

Now, Adam was standing over me where I sat, looking down and still smiling. Suddenly he bent over and picked me up. I screamed and pretended to struggle, kicking my legs until my shoes fell off. He took no notice and ran into the bedroom. How glad I was that he knew me so well... biblically, too.

3

The plane dipped its wing at an alarming angle as we began the descent to Ancona airport. Adam leaned across me to look out of the window. I had tried to persuade him not to take the middle seat, but he had refused. Adam had sat, evidently quite content, his long legs bent double with his knees touching the seat in front. Somehow he had managed to round his broad shoulders and had sat holding his iPad and scrolling happily through his photos. Now, he said,

'Look down there, blue, blue sea... I've never swum in the Adriatic.'

His face was very close to mine, and I found myself admiring his long fluffy blonde eyelashes. I brushed his cheek with a quick kiss and then said,

'I can't believe how you can endure the discomfort of this budget airline. Why did Melanie arrange such a ridiculous way for us to get to Ancona?'

Adam kissed me on the end of my nose and then settled back into his seat. 'Well, I think it's probably the only airline that flies here direct. Anyway, such a short flight, it's fine. But then, I suppose it's not up to Princess travel standard.'

I sighed and tried to ease my back away from the hard plastic seat,

'Not so short... it has seemed an eternity to me.'

'That's because you're a Princess. This is an up to date version of the Princess and the Pea story.'

I was quiet then as I suddenly thought of what long and dangerous flights he must have made in his career as a war photographer. I decided not to chastise him over referring to me as Princess. Somehow, it seemed a reasonable offence as perhaps I had been behaving right royally? My wealthy upbringing, when I had never travelled any other way than a private jet or first class, was rearing its ugly head again. Would I ever be able to behave like Adam, enjoying simple everyday events? Certainly, real royalty would be educated to carry out their duties with respect, but I had just grown up showered with money. I had been drilled to behave with good social manners and etiquette but..,

My thoughts were interrupted by Adam, leaning over me and fastening my seat belt,

'You're such a sweet dreamer, Eve. You were deep in another of your Eve-reveries, weren't you? I love watching your face when you dream off. Mostly you have this delightful Garbo-esque smile, but sometimes you draw your eyebrows into a little frown.'

I sighed, 'I don't know which is more ridiculous or annoying, calling me Princess or hanging on to your idea that I look like Greta Garbo.'

'Never mind, my love, I just can't help the Garbo thing as for calling you Princess... I know, I know, Princess Don't-be-Vulgar... but you're so beautiful when you're cross.'

'Isn't that a rather corny line?'

'Hmm, rather over-used but so apt for you.' Adam settled back into his seat and returned to flicking through his iPad. Then, laughing, he showed me the screen as he said,

'Look, how can you deny it? That's Garbo as Mata Hari, you're practically a double!'

I looked at the black and white photo of Greta Garbo and knew I should admit it was true, but I stayed silent. Adam took the iPad back and opened another file and then said,

'Look at this one then.'

Now I peered at the small screen and drew in my breath in shock. The likeness was incredible this time. Then I laughed,

'You're crazy. That is me, isn't it? You've photoshopped me into a film shot of Garbo wearing a turban.'

Adam was heaving with laughter, almost unable to speak, he muttered, 'Oh, if only you had seen the look on your face. First, you knew I was right and then, then...' He exploded with more laughter, and the young man on the other side of him turned to look at us. Adam tried to control his laughter and said, 'Then when you saw yourself as Mata Hari. Just too good, too good.'

I dug him hard in the ribs with my elbow, but it only increased his laughter. I turned away from him and looked out of the window. We were flying low now, approaching the airport. Then, I caught my reflection in the small window and saw that I was smiling, nearly laughing.

'I turned back to Adam, 'I can't think why on earth you would waste your time over such rubbish.'

'Oh, not wasted time. I enjoy messing around and need to update my skills constantly. It is my work, after all. Using your face is just pure pleasure. I only married you because you're so photogenic.'

I gave a harder dig in his ribs, and then the plane bumped, once and then again down to the earth. There was a light ripple of applause throughout the cabin.

I looked at Adam in surprise, 'Are the passengers truly applauding a journey of dire discomfort ending with a bumpy landing.'

'Oh, they often do that on budget airlines... just fun or maybe relief that they are back safely on terra firma. You'll get used to it.'

'Relief I can appreciate, but you can't believe I'll get used to it. You don't think I am ever going to travel like this again, do you?'

Adam began to laugh again, and the young man on the other side of him was already unbuckling his seatbelt even though the announcement had told us not to do so. I was now suppressing a giggle which was springing up in me. How dreadful it must have been for the young Italian to have travelled next to us. There was another reason I felt suddenly relaxed and happy. I turned to Adam and said,

'Just think how wonderful it will be to find Bernard at the airport, holding the door open to the leathery luxury of his Mercedes.'

And, as soon as we came out of the airport, there was Bernard, just as I had said, standing by the open door of his long Mercedes. I ran ahead, leaving Adam hampered with his backpack and all my luggage, and threw my arms around Bernard. I knew quite well that he would be very embarrassed, but I just couldn't resist. He put his hands on my shoulders, as though to steady me and I had the sudden thought that he was more a father to me than my real father. Then, Adam caught up with us, and Bernard turned to shake his hand as Adam said,

'Great to see you, Bernie, old man.'

'Very good to see you both again... but remember, Adam, how you get into trouble calling me old.'

'Well, I do remember you ducking me in that fountain in Frascati. Right now, I feel pretty safe though, you're parked on some sort of double yellow band and being watched by the local police... and they have guns.'

'Is OK, I know the head of the carabinieri in Ancona. No problem for the parking and I tell him that Eve is a celebrity.'

I looked around anxiously, hoping not to be recognised, but the people milling around seemed not to even notice me. It was another downside of being on television, possibly even worse than having to perform for the camera. Intrusion into my private time was hard to stand, especially as Melanie was always ordering me to smile and sign autographs. It didn't come easily to me. Then I thought I saw someone I knew, and I almost raised my hand, but the man had already disappeared into the crowd.

Bernard was holding the back door open, and so I jumped in quickly, and Adam sat in the front. I would have liked to sit beside him in the back, but I knew he wanted to continue his usual banter with Bernard. They were very good friends and on our travels had developed almost a father to son relationship. Yes, I thought to myself, Bernard was perfect surrogate father material. I relaxed into the soft leather upholstery and rested my hand on the cashmere rug that Bernard always kept for me on the back seat. Then I closed my eyes and leant my head on the head-rest. I was tired, life with Adam could be very exhausting. I was drifting into a sleepy mood when I began to listen to the two men talking in the front. As usual, They were talking about me, and so I was interested enough to stay awake.

'Mademoiselle Eve looks very well, Adam.'

'Better not let you hear you call her Mademoiselle. Remember, Bernie, she wants you to call her Eve now.'

'*C'est vrai,* very true. Is difficult after all these years.'

'I guess, but you know everything is different now. More difficult for Eve than for any of us. She has lost so much that she was accustomed to having. As for you, well, it's a great favour to us that you leave Elaine running your farmhouse venture in Roussillon. Now, you are not working for Eve but with Eve.'

'Is good to think that, Adam. But you know, the agency pay me very well for this work. Eve's father is behind it somewhere, *je suis sur.*'

I almost sat up in shock at Bernard's last words. It had been enjoyable to hear the two men in the front of the car exchanging kind words about me. I glued my eyelashes closed again, reluctant to give up on hearing more. It wasn't the first time I had eavesdropped in the same way. The old adage that eavesdroppers seldom hear anything good of themselves had never worked for me. I thought about this for a moment and drifted into thoughts of how often it was used by Shakespeare, in Hamlet for example, and, of course, Twelfth Night. I wafted onward, mentally listing other plays where the technique had been used to forward the plot. Then, there was the added possibility that the speakers knowing the eavesdropper was listening could manipulate the situation. Interesting. I would be able to write a reasonable paper on the subject if I were still studying in my little room at Cambridge. I idly imagined myself back in the cloistered life I had led, wondering how it would have been if I had taken up the offer of a fellowship. Did I regret anything? I almost shook my head to dismiss my own question, but I managed to stay very still, feigning deeper sleep. Had I missed anything while I had been lost in what Adam called my Eve-reveries?

Bernard was speaking quietly,

'That last meeting we had at Brown's, after our work in Kent, that was very good for Eve, I think.'

'You mean when we met up with the amazing Entwhistle sisters? Yes, you're right, Bernie. I think something melted in Eve that day and she allowed herself to forgive her father... at least a little.'

'*C'est vrai, à pardonner et oublier...* how you say, forgive and forget?'

'Exactly, you know, Bernie old boy, your English is finally improving.'

'I hope there is a very big fountain at our new hotel... is time I gave you another lesson in swimming.'

'*Pardon et oubli* something, *nestle par*, Bernie?'

Bernie gave one of his rare low chuckles, 'And your French remains terrible. But you are fortunate this time. I think the villa where we are staying has not the fountain. Melanie Powers sent me the details, and I do not see any water hazards in the gardens.'

'Villa? Are we staying in a private villa, like the one in Tuscany?'

'No, I think more a big house that the owners now run as a ... I am not sure of the word.... hostel, *peutêtre?*'

At this, I could no longer bear to pretend to be asleep. What had Melanie arranged? I had been so busy in the few days before we left London that I hadn't bothered to check out our hotel arrangements. Hostel? For goodness sakes! I may have managed to change some of my ways, adjusting to my new working life, but surely Melanie knew by now that I demanded five-star luxury? Hadn't the flight been bad enough? I made a show of waking and stretching, and Adam immediately turned around.

'The beautiful Princess awakes, and I haven't even kissed her.' He leant over and tousled my hair.

I smoothed it over again and said, 'Do you really think you can play the part of the dashing Prince... in that old Parka?'

'Ah, but you forget that I was once a frog until you kissed me.'

Adam and I often had these ridiculous conversations, and they usually ended in a row or bed, or both. Now was not the time. I didn't want to admit to eavesdropping, so I casually said,

'Are we nearly at our hotel now, Bernard? Are we nearly there?'

My last words had a familiar childish ring. How many thousand times must I have asked Bernard the same question?

'*Bien sur...* er... Eve,' I knew very well that Bernard had been about to call me Mademoiselle and that Adam had coughed a warning. I smiled at their boyish collusion. As if I minded what Bernard called me. What I did mind, very much mind, was the idea that we were heading toward some hostel. Then Bernard added,

'*Et voilà, nous sommes arrivés.* Here we are! The Villa Adriana'

I looked out of the window as Bernard drove very slowly up a smooth gravel road between an avenue of tall cypress trees. Between the dark trunks of the trees, I caught glimpses, of the sparkling blue sea in the distance. I looked ahead, peering between Adam and Bernard, and saw an impressive and perfectly symmetrical villa ahead. Its coral coloured walls and light grey shutters were pale from years of sunshine. I relaxed and remained silent. Why had I not trusted Melanie? Yes, this classic 17th-century villa had distinct five-star possibilities. Bernard drew into the circular driveway and turned to Adam.

'*Quelle chance!* Is a beautiful palace, *non? Et regarde!* A very large fountain.'

'Have to catch me first, old man!' Adam jumped out of the car the moment it stopped and headed off into the gardens, waving his camera aloft.

5

'It's not what I'd call a villa, it's more a palace.'
Adam spoke as he looked through the viewfinder of his camera.

'Well, 'villa' is a word that has changed its identity since Roman times.'

'Hmm, that's just the sort of answer I would expect from you, clever clogs. But to me, a villa is some sort of spiv's hideaway in Benidorm.'

I sighed and decided that it was impossible to explain the evolution of the villa from the Roman Empire through the years leading to the style of the 17th century Villa Adriana. It was much too pleasant, wandering hand in hand with Adam through the impeccable gardens, for a history lesson.

'When you sigh like that, my sweet Princess, you make me very aware of my shortcomings.'

'Shortcomings? How can you say that... or are you fishing for compliments? Worse, are you going for a play on words?'

Adam threw back his head and roared with laughter.

'What a devious mind you have, my love. Is there a word 'longcomings?'

I leaned into him as we walked, having admired his strong throat and the early evening sunlight caught in his dark blonde hair. Irresistible and perfect example of manhood, I thought to myself but said,

'There isn't such a word, but there should be. Perfect noun to describe what we have together.'

'You little minx! You're doing your clever poetry stuff, aren't you? How you do love words.' Adam laughed again and squeezed me hard, 'Wouldn't longcomings be an improper noun, Professor Sinclair?'

Now I was laughing, too as I said, 'Common noun is the term, I think.'

'Oh, here we go, now you're really getting into academic mode. When you make a statement and add that 'I think', it's when you're very sure of yourself but would like an argument.'

'Don't be ridiculous, Adam, I say it when I don't want to push a known fact home too hard. It's just being polite.'

Adam drew me over to a long stone bench and sank down onto it, pulling me onto his lap.

'Can't you say anything right now that doesn't have a sexy double meaning? Push home? You're a wicked minx. If I lay down along this bench would you consider my shortcomings and improperly push home?'

Wrapped in his arms, I could feel his body responding to mine. I nestled into the curve of his shoulders and inhaled the perfume that always hung around him. A top note of sweet herbs and yet there was a faint, elusive aroma of the sea and a distinct end-tone of peppermint. I pressed my highly trained nose into the hollow of his right collarbone. Why could I never quite distinguish the ingredients? Then I felt Adam laughing,

'Are you sniffing me again, Princess? You're like a little animal nuzzling at me. I've told you before, anything pleasant you smell on me is just soap and toothpaste. Now, behave yourself, please. We should continue our rounds of the gardens and go in for dinner.'

I stood up reluctantly, 'I know, we're meeting Bernard in half an hour, but you do have the most delicious clavicles.'

Adam was laughing again as he stood up and took my hand to continue our stroll, 'Now, I've heard everything... delicious clavicles. Only you, Eve, only you...'

I interrupted him, 'Informally known as saltcellars, I believe. The hollows each end of your collarbone. Yours are beautiful, deep and perfectly delicious.'

'Stop, please stop, Princess, or we shall never get to dinner, and we can't desert Bernard on his first night here. Believe me, I shall return to the subject later and give you a serious lesson on your many delicious bumps and deep hollows.' Adam gave me another squeeze and added, 'Now, please behave yourself.'

'Very well, I'll try, but I think the soft, warm air blowing in from the Adriatic is having its effect on me. I feel so relaxed.'

'Me, too. It is the most beautiful place. I bet it has a history of canoodling lovers strolling along its pathways. We must thank Melanie for searching out the Villa Adriana.'

'Canoodling, what a beautiful word, Adam. It describes exactly what we are doing. Maybe there is a remnant of romance in the gardens here, although I am sure it was built as a hunting lodge. Perhaps there was time for dalliance in between killing animals for fun?' I looked up the steps ahead of us, leading to the front terrace and added, 'The restoration work is tremendously good, the whole place is set back in time. Our suite is glorious and room service very discreet. Yes, I'll thank Melanie. I was worried when Bernard said he thought it was a hostel.'

'As if Melanie would dare book you into a hostel. Now, there's a word I do know. I've stayed in the worst hostels all over the world.'

'Hmm, but then the word '*hôtellerie'* in French, the circumflex substituting the letter 's', or rather suppressing the preconsonantal 's' is...'

Adam suddenly stopped walking and stood still in front of me, his light blue eyes looking at me seriously,

'Eve, do you miss your life as an academic?'

'Good Heavens, no! Of course not. I've never been happier in my entire life.'

Adam smiled down at me, 'I hope so, my love. I will do anything in the world to make you happy.'

'Then just keep as you are, please, putting up with my many princessy shortcomings in getting to grips with the reality of life… and enjoying our longcomings.'

We walked on again through a trellised pergola of perfumed pink roses. I looked up at the blue sky between the delicate flowers and glossy green leaves.

Was this walk a metaphor for our life ahead? But I said nothing more.

I was happy, so happy to realise that it was true. I didn't miss my former arid, erudite life one scrap.

6

We were halfway through our elegant dinner in the perfectly round salon in the west wing of the Villa Adriana. Bernard was sitting between us, solid as a rock in his immaculate navy blue blazer. We had caught up with all his news about Elaine and her new language school. Then we had reminisced about our time there when I was researching for my chapter on the sweet wine of Roussillon.

'It's such a beautiful part of France and Elaine's farmhouse has a similar distant view of the sea as we have here from the Villa.' I gazed out of the long open window beside our table as I spoke. The horizon of the Adriatic was shimmering into the mauves and pinks of a dramatic sunset.

'Of all our assignments, this is our tenth now, I enjoyed staying in your farmhouse best of all.' Adam stopped eating for a moment, nodded and then continued his progress through a large T-bone steak.

'True,' I agreed, Elaine is a wonderful hostess, Bernard.'

'*C'est vrai*, very true. I am the lucky man, *bien sur*!'

Suddenly I sat back in my chair, 'Oh my goodness, I've only just remembered. I'm sure I saw Johnny Harrington at the airport.'

Adam stopped eating again and looked at me with his eyebrows raised, 'The lovely Johnny-Gianni? Are you sure?'

'Yes, although he disappeared quickly into the crowds. But I'm sure it was him. Although it seems strange that he would be so far off his comfort zone in their Castello in Tuscany.'

'Maybe you were mistaken. Or maybe he was a romantic vision. You had quite a thing for him when we had our assignment there.'

I sat up straight, 'I did not have what you call a thing about Johnny Harrington, most definitely not.'

'Don't protest too much, my love, or I shall have to seek him out and challenge him to a punch-up.'

'You're being ridiculous so just stop. Even if it was Johnny, we're not likely to bump into him again. Now, please pass me the salt. I need just a little sprinkling on this grilled fish.'

'Do you mean the salt-cellar, my love?' Adam passed me the little silver salt pot and, at the same time rested his hand on my knee under cover of the long white tablecloth.

Bernard had been sitting quietly, as he always did when Adam and I began one of our ridiculously silly conversations or mini-arguments. Now, he held up his hand to us, and half stood up as he said,

'Mon Dieu, regardez-vous! Is Johnny Harrington and Rowena.'

Adam and I turned around and there, indeed, was the impeccably handsome Johnny and his girlfriend, Rowena. I remembered how we had bumped into them in Florence outside Dante's house when they were on an art tour of the city. Perhaps Johnny was the sort of person that one did come across... some friends and acquaintances seemed to follow a pattern of coincidence. Now, surprised as I was to bump into them again, I was even more surprised to see the large bump of advanced pregnancy under Rowena's linen smock.

We all stood up then and went to meet them as they came into the centre of the dining salon. As we had previously been the only diners, there was room for our enthusiastic greetings. Johnny lent down and kissed me three times on my cheeks, and I caught Adam's eye upon me. I frowned and glared at him and then moved on to greet Rowena.

'This is a wonderful surprise, Rowena... not just meeting here but...look at you! When is your baby due?'

'Lovely to see you again, Eve. Another two months yet even though I look so huge.'

Rowena blushed prettily and looked at Johnny as though for confirmation or maybe congratulation? He immediately put his arm across her shoulders in the way that Italian men often walk with their partners, was it protective or possessive? I was thinking about this when Adam came over to me and slipped his around my waist, probably possessive and definitely loving.

Bernard arranged for our table to be laid for two more, and we all sat down, still exchanging news. The sunset had changed to that soft twilight before the stars began to stud the sky. I looked across the gardens, admiring the statuary and formal topiary in this new half-light of dusk. Then, I saw a figure running in and out of the trees at the edge of the small forest below the grounds of the villa. I gave a start of alarm. There was something furtive about the way the man ran, low to the ground and keeping to the shadows. Adam was chatting with Rowena, but Bernard noticed my sudden concentrated observation.

'You see something. Mademoiselle Eve?' He turned around to follow the direction of my gaze, but the man had disappeared into the darkness of the dense trees.

I shook my head slowly, 'I don't think so, not really. I thought I saw a man but anyway, probably a gardener or even a poacher... maybe a ghost? The forest would have once been a hunting ground, I'm sure.'

I smiled at Bernard to reassure him. I knew he had once been employed by my father as my bodyguard as well as chauffeur. It was a role that Bernard found impossible to change and very often, even on our wine trips, I had occasion to be very grateful to him. Now, I wanted him to enjoy the rest of his dinner, and I dismissed all thought of my glimpse of the man acting somewhat suspiciously.

I dismissed the thought, but only after reflecting that I had been right about seeing Johnny in the crowd at the airport.

7

I awoke late. I knew it as soon as I opened my eyes and saw the sunshine glinting through the slats of the shutters. It was not the soft light of early morning, and there was a large space in the bed beside me. This was not unusual as Adam needed so little sleep and loved to be out with his camera as soon as day broke. I yawned and stretched, checked the time on my mobile and found it was nearly nine. I reluctantly pulled myself out of the comfort of the large bed. Late as it was, I could have slept for another hour at least. We had stayed up past midnight, chatting with Johnny and Rowena. They were good company and very happy together. Adam had been fascinated by the idea of them about to have a baby and plied Rowena with questions. She was a very natural, sweet girl and enjoyed his enthusiasm. I had watched Johnny as they spoke and was relieved to see he was excited with the thought of being a father. They both seemed to have matured since we last met and had solid plans for their future. Johnny had found work in an art gallery in London and escaped from his wealthy life in the Harringtons' Castello in Tuscany. I could identify with the way he had forged his own life. Yes, I thought now, as I went back through the conversation of the evening, Johnny Harrington was now quite another story.

I was in the shower when I heard Adam come back into our suite.

'Are you waiting for me in the shower, my wicked vixen-wife?'

In answer, I turned the lock on the shower room door and continued washing my hair. Today had already started late, and we had to work. I closed my eyes and let the strong jets of hot water stream over me. Everything at the Villa Adriana celebrated the 17th century except the state-of-the-art plumbing. Then, I flicked my eyes open and gave a small scream of shock as Adam walked into the torrent of water and took me in his arms.

'But, I locked the door!' It was all I could think to say before succumbing to his gentle massage, first running his fingers through the shampoo in my hair and then following the foam as it ran down my body. I stretched my arms up and pulled his head down so that I could kiss him and then said,

'Buongiorno, mio caro marito! Why are you so irresistible and irrepressible?'

'Only because I love you so much.' His voice was low and husky, and I circled his body with my legs as he lifted me up. We made urgent and fast love under the torrent of water and as soon as it was over, Adam wrapped me in a large towel and carried me into the bedroom. He lay me carefully on the bed and looked down at me,

'Would you let me take your photo, wrapped up like that and with your eyes so dreamy?'

'Definitely not! Don't you dare.'

'It would be strictly for me only.'

'No, no, no.'

'But I thought you said I was irresistible.'

'That doesn't mean I can't resist everything you want to do.'

'What about the irrepressible bit? What did you mean?'

'Nothing stops you, does it? How did you get through a locked door?'

Adam laughed and turned away from me to look out of the window, 'Surely I've told you enough about my mis-spent youth to make that an unnecessary question? Now, you won't want to hear this, but I can see Bernard already outside with the car.'

I jumped up off the bed and said,

'This is all your fault, Adam Wright. I was already late before you joined me in the shower. Now my legs feel like jelly.'

Adam turned back to me, 'Can I feel them? Sounds interesting and I love the way you said I joined you. You see, it's all your fault, you beguile me with words.'

Now he was pulling on his jeans and t-shirt. As he bent to put on his shoes and socks, I sneaked a look at his muscled back and the way his hair fell forward. I sighed, yes, positively irresistible and irrepressible.

'I heard your little sigh. Don't worry, I'm ready, I'll go down and tell Bernard we need another hour for breakfast. You'd better eat something before we set off for work.'

'Have you had breakfast?'

'Well, I made my way into the kitchens as I was starving at five-thirty this morning. A very nice woman gave me a hunk of bread and some honey. But I am more than ready for a second breakfast now.'

'You have an irrepressible appetite in all things, Adam.'

'Does that have another of your second meanings?'

'Probably. Did you get some good photos?'

'Do you think I don't know when you're changing the subject? But yes, it's natural beauty all around. I had a quick swim...'

'Swim? But it looks miles down to the beach.'

'Not as far as it looks if you go in a straight line. I made my way through the forest.'

I was about to tell him about the man I had seen skulking along the edge of the trees, but now I just had to get dressed. Adam continued,

'I only had a quick dip as I had left my camera in my Parka on the shingle. I was keeping an eye on it all the time, and I went back to shore when I saw a suspicious looking guy walking down from the woods.'

I made a mental note to tell him later about the man I had seen. Then, I forgot all about it.

After a fine breakfast and an apology to Bernard, we set off over an hour late for our appointment with the wine-grower near Jesi. Bernard had called ahead to say we were running late, something he had often done before. I know he would have made a good reason and not said that I had been late getting up. Or too long in the shower, I thought to myself and enjoyed a moment of recall. Then I sat forward and said,

'Thank you for calling the Casa Verde, Bernard. Did they mind?'

'Non, non, I spoke to the son, and he was very friendly and relaxed. He spoke the good English and, when I apologised, he replied 'cool.'

'Cool?' Adam repeated, sounds like a young man who has spent time in the UK or the States. Makes it easier for me. It's all right for you, Eve, you speak the lingo.'

'My Italian is not as good as my French, but I studied Dante and Leopardi in the original texts, of course.'

'Of course,' Adam tried to mimic my voice in a silly falsetto, and I decided to ignore him. Too often our car journeys turned into a small fight of words. Then Adam rested his hand on my knee and said in his own voice, 'So tell me, where are you taking me this time, my Princess Clever Clogs?'

I also ignored the annoying way he called me Princess, it was too repetitive to tell him off every time and, I had to admit to myself, I was beginning to like it or at least not mind.

I rested my hand over his and caught a glimpse of the sparkle of my engagement ring and the narrow gold band of my wedding ring. I had a surge of energy or maybe happiness as I thought about our day ahead.

'I think it will be interesting and you'll find some great opportunities for photos. The vines stretched down a steep slope… it's so high that there is a vast panorama and you can see the sea. I've only looked at their website, but some years ago I tasted their white Verdicchio dei Castelli di Jesi. I remember it distinctly, so fresh and fruity with a slight lemony undertone, but not too acidic… or shouldn't be, depending on the vintage.'

'How on earth can you remember a wine you tasted years ago? No, don't answer that... what's the name of the place?'

'Case Verde.'

'Is that with an 'e' or an 'i'?

'Ends with 'e' like the colour green not like the composer.'

'Of course, Verrday.' Adam mimicked my voice again, and I gave him the usual jab in his ribs with my elbow. As usual, he ignored it and was concentrating on his iPad. Then he raised his eyebrows at me,

'Casa Verde comes up as a venture capital company specialising in the cannabis industry. Where are you taking me, my love?'

'Don't be ridiculous, Adam.' Then I sat forward to speak to Bernard who usually chose to keep quiet as he drove. 'Bernard, do you have the Casa Verde address?'

'*Bien sur*, already I have checked the route and now is in the sat-nav. Is nothing to do with the company Adam finds. *Comme meme*, I telephoned with my friend in the Carabinieri in Ancona last night, He say there is a very, very big drug problem here in his area. Many associated crimes, too. He warned me to be very careful. Is not all beautiful mountains and blue of the Adriatica, I think. Look under Jesi, Adam.'

'S'OK, found it now. Oh yes, looks fantastic. Lousy website, though. Photos could definitely be improved by a guy like me. Or by me, as there is no-one as good as me, of course. I wonder if they ever get confused with the finance company?'

'Only by people like you, I imagine, egoistic idiots. Anyway, Casa Verde interests me just because they have do have a low profile and sell mostly in Italy. Melanie told me that they want to export more and I've been invited to taste and sign their new label.'

'Let's hope you still like it then. This egoist idiot hopes so, anyway.' Adam closed his eyes and rested his head back on the headrest. I restrained from running my fingers through his long curls, still damp from our shower.

'I hope so, too, and if it's how I remember it, then I shall be happy to recommend it and add my signature. If not...' I paused and Adam, sitting close beside me, opened one eye and frowned at me. I continued, 'If not, there is another Verdicchio region around Matelica, the other side of the Monti Sibillini, a high range of the Apennines. Interesting difference in the same grape in the two areas, for example...'

Adam now pretended to snore, so I gave up and added, 'Anyway, I think the wine from Casa Verde will be great.'

Adam was still pretending to be asleep, so I leaned forward again to speak to Bernard.

'You've had long days of driving, Bernard. All the way from Banyuls-sur-Mer. Are you tired?'

'*Mais non,* Mademoiselle Eve, is my usual work and the journey was fast on A routes.'

'Sorry, we were so late. Did you have an early breakfast?'

'Yes, very fine breakfast, *merci*, Mademoiselle.'

'Would you like a chocolate? There was a little box in our room, and I put them in my bag. Mmm, handmade, very stylish chocolates... strawberry cream?'

'OK, OK,' Adam opened both eyes and sat forward, 'I give up, did you say chocolate? I was so nearly asleep.'

'Hmm, funny how the mention of chocolate woke you up.'

I offered the bag to Adam, and he carefully selected the largest one and then looked at me as he said,

'It wasn't the word 'chocolate', it was that Bernard called you Mademoiselle twice and you never told him off. Do you want this big chocolate, my love?' He held the chocolate aloft, and I shook my head.

'I know Bernard doesn't even eat chocolate so that means I can eat it.' He popped the chocolate into his mouth, gave a blissful smile, closed his eyes again and mumbled with his mouth full,

'Mmm, irresistible!'

9

Bernard pulled up in front of a long white-painted farmhouse. We had driven up a steep hill, with rows of vines on each side and Adam was already excited at the view.

As usual, he jumped out of the Mercedes before Bernard had quite driven to a halt.

'Great place, Eve, another good fine of yours.' He flung out his arms as though to embrace the panorama and added, 'I have a good feeling about this place.'

Bernard opened my door for me, and I stepped out, breathing in the fresh air. I knew that Adam's enthusiasm was partly because he was hoping that the wines of Casa Verde would meet my approval. Otherwise, as had happened before, we would be back in the car, searching the area for another wine-grower. Much as Adam enjoyed our work together in the vineyards of Europe, he was now involved with a new project in London and had left it in charge of his business partner, my ex-school friend, Lucinda Sackville-Jones. I turned in a circle, admiring the 350-degree view that encompassed the distant turquoise horizon of the Adriatic and around to the misty lavender blue of the Sibillini mountains. It was breath-taking, and I thought how far it all seemed from our loft in Clerkenwell... and Lucinda who would about now be opening up the new studio in Plaistow.

I was proud of Adam's work and his aim to get underprivileged kids off the street and involved with photography. It was already very successful and, had also saved Lucinda. I knew she was probably in love with Adam and in thrall to his talent, a society photographer herself but from a background which couldn't have been more different to Adam's. I had been at school with her but lost touch when I went up to Cambridge. Lucinda, always a party girl had moved in a very wrong set in London and ended up in rehab at the Priory. I smiled to myself, thinking how I had almost been jealous of Lucinda when she began to worship at Adam's feet. There was nothing for me to worry about and a lot to be very glad about. Adam had saved Lucinda by offering her serious work, something she had never tried before. He trusted her, and she had repaid him by working conscientiously at the new studio. I was almost sure that my father had invested in the project.

I turned around again, taking a deep breath of the air that came from the mountains and the sea. Enough dreaming, now I should get down to work.

I turned back to look at the farmhouse building and saw a young man emerging, pushing his long black hair back from his face as he advanced toward us. The bright sunlight lit his dark Italian face, and he smiled and held out his arms in greeting. Quite a dramatic entrance, I thought, as I walked toward him.

'*Benvenuti*, welcome to Casa Verde!' His voice was something of a disappointment, high pitched and thin, and his fine long nose was red-tipped. Maybe he wouldn't make a movie star then. We shook hands, and I said,

'Thank you, what a wonderful place you have here. It's like the top of the world.'

The young man looked around as though he had never noticed the view before, then with a slight shrug of his elegant shoulders, he nodded,

'Yeah, cool.'

I thought this was a slight understatement but said nothing as now Adam was introducing himself,

'Hi, my name's Adam Wright.'

'I'm Luigi Marioni, pleased to meet you. No need to introduce yourself with your reputation as a celebrity photographer. I went to your exhibition in Paris. Cool!'

They shook hands, and then Bernard stepped forward and silently shook the young man's hand. We began to move toward the farmhouse entrance. I was already hoping that Luigi Marioni would not be part of our visit. Cool indeed? How could he use that silly teenage word to comment on Adam's beautiful and yet horrendous war photos? Adam was following me, and he quickly stroked my back as he had guessed I was seething with silent rage. He rested his hand on my shoulder and whispered,

'He's only a kid, really, hiding under his designer clothes and lost in his Gucci loafers.' I exhaled sharply and tried to agree, and Adam continued,

'Be cool, Princess Un-Cool.'

Then, I almost giggled and found my anger subsiding as we went into the dark hall of the farmhouse.

10

'So, were the wines good enough to write home about, Eve?'

We were seated beside each other in the back of the Mercedes and heading downhill from Casa Verde. I hesitated long enough to enjoy the small wrinkle in Adam's tanned forehead, then nodded,

'Their Verdicchio Riserva is superb.'

Adam gave an audible sigh of relief, and I caught Bernard's eye in the driving mirror, and we both smiled. How often had I exchanged glances with Bernard in this complicit way? Since I was a child, or at least since I was tall enough to see over the front seat? Now, Bernard gave an almost imperceptible nod, and I continued happily,

'Did you get any good photos?'

'What a question to ask me, Princess. Naturally, I have taken at least forty cracking shots. Look for yourself. You can pick some if you want.'

Adam passed me his camera, and even on the small screen, I could tell he was not bragging. In every frame, the sky was a luminous blue, and it was hard to choose between the vineyards stretching uphill toward the mountains or downhill to the sea. Apart from which, I knew from experience that Adam would spend hours going through them later and the choice would be his alone. It was how it should be, the writing was quite enough for me.

'They do look splendid, Adam, thank you. Looks like this might be an easy assignment. I have plenty to write about even though the young Luigi wasn't much help. I think he must have had a bad head cold. He kept sniffing, and his perfect Roman nose was quite red.'

Adam took back his camera and spoke absent-mindedly,

'Yes, well, you did realise that he was well out of it?'

'What do you mean, out of it?'

Adam turned to face me, and his light blue eyes were disconcertingly sad as he said,

'High as a kite. Didn't you realise? Nice kid, really but well... just a shame.'

'You mean he was under the influence of a drug of some sort?'

'Well, that's the way you'd put it... I'd say his brain is either fried already or half-baked. I was hoping his parents might turn up. I wonder if they can do anything?'

'Are you sure, Adam, I know you like to be the saviour saint of youngsters on the wrong path, but Luigi Marioni is hardly one of your deprived kids off a sink estate.'

'As if that makes a jot of difference. Really, Eve, you should think about what you say. Sometimes your Princess behaviour goes too far.'

I sat quietly, feeling angry and yet a little ashamed. I had just thought that Luigi had been incredibly vague or maybe going down with a cold, or suffering from hay-fever. He had hurriedly shown us down to the cellars and then let us wander through the vineyards unaccompanied. Now, thinking about it, it did seem likely that he had been under the influence of something I knew little about. Even my time at Cambridge had done little to educate me in the doubtful joys of the weed. I had soon found that parties were held in a sweet haze and just stopped going when invited. Soon, the invitations had dropped away and, apart from my few Wine Club friends, I had stayed mostly on my own. When I became serious about becoming a Master of Wine, I guarded my palate like the crown jewels. I knew I had a good memory, but it was the taste buds that finally counted and nothing that could be learned from a book. Now, I was pleased that the Verdicchio I had tasted several years before, even though a different vintage, had the same excellent quality. Yes definitely worth writing about. I decided to ignore Adam's jibe and said,

'I must say, I was hoping to get to speak with someone more knowledgeable. Luigi said his father was sailing on his yacht somewhere off Corsica or maybe the Greek islands. I suppose it's a good time for him to go, before the work of the harvest. But still...'

Adam closed his iPad and looked at me again as he said.

'But still, it's a great shame. These rich boys, like Johnny-Gianni, too, what dreadful childhoods they had to endure.'

'Your own childhood was hardly idyllic, how can you feel sorry for them?'

'Oh, but, but I do. The neglect of rich parents is something else, you should know that. My Mum died, and that was that. My old man took to the bottle, and I was allowed to run wild. Still, I had a right old time playing with the gipsy lads in the Lea Valley. Never having a Mum to tell me I never should etc. Then, I had two amazing teachers at secondary, somehow they saw something of value in me. That's all it takes, don't you think?'

I was beginning to feel out of my emotional depth with so many ideas churning in my head. Neglected? I took a deep breath and decided to change the subject to more familiar ground.

'Luigi thought his father might be back before the end of the week, so I'll try and meet him. Whether they were good parents or not, they certainly know how to make wine.'

'Do one of your juicy descriptions, Eve, tell me all about it, like… once upon a time on a hill near the Adriatic...'

I looked at Adam suspiciously as he usually didn't encourage me to talk wine.

'Do you really want to know?'

Adam nodded and settled his head back on the headrest.

I continued with enthusiasm, 'Firstly, the vines are organically grown, truly organic and not a pretence. The soil is limestone-rich clay and the high altitude, rising about four hundred metres above sea level, preserves the acidity during the growing season. The grapes are picked and pressed immediately, then fermented at a low temperature. I'm going to check, but I think the wine tanks are left outside in the winter for a natural and mild stabilisation. So interesting., don't you think?'

I turned to Adam and saw he was sound asleep and not even pretending.

11

We had arranged to meet Johnny and Rowena for dinner at the Villa that evening. I had spent longer than usual on dressing and sweeping my hair into a high pleat. I looked into the mirror over the dressing table and frowned critically at my image. Earrings or not? I held some long dangling opals up to my ears and then shook my head at myself. No, I decided, enough effort had already been made. My pleated Issey Miyake dress was a sufficient statement. I stood up and admired the way that the silk pleats followed my body. Yes, quite good. I saw that Adam was watching me in the mirror and smiling. Then, he said,

'Shall we go dallying again in the gardens before dinner, Eve?'

'That would be nice.' I looked doubtfully down at my fragile, high-heeled Louboutin sandals. The pale blonde leather fitted softly to my toes, and the thin ankle straps made them easy to walk in. Easier, anyway. The height of the narrow straight heels was not designed for strolling on gravel paths.

Adam stood beside me and looked down, 'Well, you can't wear your Loubies, they're made for strutting not walking.'

'You're so into fashion, it always surprises me. How do you know my sandals are Christian Louboutin?'

'Please... give me a break! I've told you I spent two years as a fashion photographer. Shooting the chicest on the world's top catwalks. I lived with fashion.'

'Hmm, you mean you lived with fashion models.' I gave him a light kick in his shin with the toe of my sandal.

'Well, there were some dalliances.'

'That's your new word, isn't it? Dalliance?'

'Well, you used it yesterday, and I try to learn, you know. Anyway, I do think it's a very fine word, my high-heeled Princess Dilly-Dally.'

I looked into Adam's eyes as he stood close to me, 'I'm nearly as tall as you in these sandals.'

'Apart from the fact I can still see over your head, sure thing. Now, why not take off your sandals and I'll keep them in my Parka pockets. You can wear your loafers and change before we meet up with the young and glamorous young Harrington.'

'I'm not worried about looking good for Johnny Harrington.' I said indignantly while bending down to unbuckle my ankle straps.

'That is such a blatant lie, Eve, and you know it. Here let me.'

Adam knelt down and unbuckled both straps of my shoes, gently caressing each foot before placing it on the silky carpet. How his touch melted me. I looked down and stroked my hand lightly across his dark blonde curls. He looked up at me, his light blue eyes darkening with intent as he ran his hand up my leg. I knew that look so well and said hastily,

'There's not time, later, later please.'

Adam nodded and stood up, giving me a rueful, slightly crooked smile and said, 'I'll find your old loafers, then.'

Soon after, walking hand in hand through the paths of the formal gardens, I could still feel the residue of longing deep inside me. Adam gave my arm a squeeze, as though sensing my emotion and said,

'Isn't it just the best thing about marriage, Eve? You know, there is always to be a later... years and years of laters, stretching ahead of us.'

I rested my head on his shoulder and sighed happily, 'Yes, true. Just the opposite of a dalliance.'

'Really... what does a dalliance mean then?'

'A casual, fleeting relationship, usually, but not always sexual. An archaic word for flirtation? It comes from the Middle English word, ... though I suppose originally from the Old French 'dalier' meaning to chat... yes, dally as in dawdle plus ance, meaning conversation, of course.'

Adam threw back his head and roared with laughter, 'Of course it is! What a lucky guy I am to be married to a beautiful walking dictionary.'

I shrugged, 'More of an encyclopedia, actually.'

'And how I love the way you say, ackchewally. So hoity-toity. Lucinda says it just the same way. Must have been your posh schooling.'

I decided to ignore this and said,

'I was thinking about Lucinda today. It's great she is so dedicated to your photographic club. It's changed her life.'

'Well, she is a grand photographer, you know. When she took to the bottle, she found her hands were shaking and she couldn't work any more. Now she's fine again. She called me today.'

'Did she? You didn't say.'

'Just forgot. It was when I was roaming around the vineyards at Casa Verde. She sent you her love.'

'Hmm. Any news?' I spoke as casually as I could, struggling to hide a tinge of jealousy.

'Err, not really. She began to say she'd met up with your Dad, but then the line dropped.'

'My father's in London?' I blinked in surprise as the last time I had heard from him, he was back in India, involved in his new project of establishing a green tourist resort in Kerala. 'Still in London?' I repeated but before Adam could reply there was a voice from the rose pergola calling out,

'*Buona sera! Vieni qua, vieni qua! Sono qui...* we are in your Garden of Eden. Adam and Eve, join us here! Ro and I need help drinking this innocent grape juice.'

'*Ciao, Gianni!*' Adam called back and then turned to me in a quieter voice, 'Here's Johnny! Dallying with Rowena in amongst the roses. Come on, let's join them, Eve.'

Adam took my hand and pulled me along while I thought to myself that I sincerely hoped

Johnny was not dallying with the very pregnant Rowena. Then, I breathed in the sweet perfume of the roses and let Adam walk ahead of me with my sandals in his pockets.

12

Johnny and Rowena were sitting comfortably on a cushioned seat in the rose arbour. There was a tray set on the table in front of them with glasses and a large terracotta pitcher. Johnny stood up as we approached and leaned down to kiss me on both cheeks, making me wish that I had the advantage of Louboutin heels. I quickly sat beside Rowena, tucking my loafers under the seat as we exchanged greetings.

'Such a beautiful dress, Eve,' Rowena said, 'Is it real Issey?'

I nodded and said, 'You look wonderful, Rowena.' She blushed with delight. It was true, Rowena held all the legendary beauty of a pregnant woman. Her skin was glowing, her hair shone, and there was an air of calm around her, an aura of contentment. She sat with one hand resting gently on the sloping rise of her stomach, just under her swelling breasts. A perfect 21st-century Madonna. Just as I thought it, Johnny said,

'Don't you think Ro makes a perfect Madonna, Adam? Would you take her portrait while we're staying here?'

'My pleasure,' Adam said quickly, 'Why not right now? It would be hard to think of a more beautiful setting, and the sun is slanting down... yes.' He reached into his pocket and absent-mindedly passed me my sandal while he took out his camera. I stood, dangling the shoe from one hand and laughed at the surprise on Rowena's face as she said,

'How lovely! Does Adam always carry your spare shoes around for you?'

Johnny took in the scene and said hastily, 'I can always carry your shoes if you want, Ro, any time.'

'I know, my love, but right now there's no need as I wear flats.' She stretched out her legs and showed her pale gold pumps. I saw Johnny looking at them as though fascinated. He was most certainly in love.

Then, Adam began rearranging the scene, moving the table and turning Rowena so that the evening sunlight slanted across her. Then, he replaced her hand on her stomach and pulled a strand of her long hair over her shoulder. I had never seen him in this particular photographic mode before, and I was impressed. I had already realised the strength of his work came from his clever use of light and dark, the chiaroscuro of all great masters. Then I saw that now the sunlight glinted on a wedding ring on Rowena's hand. So they were married? I drew in my breath in delight and turned to Johnny.

'I didn't know you two were married, Johnny.'
'Of course, we are married, Eve. I'm the luckiest man on earth. When Rowena accepted me... well, it was the proudest moment of my life.'

I nodded and smiled, thinking how different a man he was from the arrogant Romeo I had met in Tuscany. What was it Adam had said? It just takes someone to believe in you? Then Rowena turned to me,

'Sorry we didn't ask you both to the wedding, but it was a very small family affair in the chapel on the Harrington estate. Oh, sorry, Adam, did I move?'

'No, it was perfect when you turned to look up at Eve. I think I have the shot.'

I was about to ask more about their wedding, but Johnny picked up the jug and said, 'Juice of the grape, anyone? Don't worry, Eve, no need to analyse it, it's innocent juice. Now we're pregnant, I've given up alcohol altogether.

He filled the glasses and Adam raised his to Rowena, then to Johnny and then smiled at me over the rim of the glass as he said, 'And that says everything we should raise a toast to. Here's to Rowena, the beautiful Madonna and to you, Johnny-Gianni, newly-wed and new-born man.'

Bernard was waiting for us at the entrance of the Villa as we returned for dinner.

'*Bonsoir*, Bernard, I hope we haven't kept you waiting.' As I spoke, I wondered how many hours Bernard must have spent waiting for me.

'Pas de tout, not at all. I wanted to ask you a favour.' Bernard smiled and looked unusually uneasy.

'Of course, what is it?' I replied quickly.

'If you think not to need me this evening... well, naturally it is not important but...'

'Bernard, you must take the evening off, absolutely. I don't need the car at all. Adam and I will eat here and have an early night. Absolutely no problem.'

'Having a night out on the town? Bernie? Hitting the hot spots of Ancona?' Adam laughed and slapped Bernard on his back. Then added with a cheeky smile, 'Don't drink and drive, old man.'

Bernard frowned, 'You see the fountain so near us, Adam?'

Adam quickly stood behind me, still laughing, 'OK, OK, calm down, old boy. I know you're a seriously married man now. Don't worry, I shan't tell your Elaine that you took off into the Italian night.'

Bernard looked threateningly at Adam and took a step towards him. Adam threw his arms around me and said, 'If I go in the fountain then your Mademoiselle Eve is coming with me... and I have her new shoes in my pocket. Mademoiselle will most certainly not want her new Loubies soaked.'

Adam picked me up and retreated backwards. I wriggled and said,

'Do stop larking around, Adam. Put me down at once.'

Rowena and Johnny were both standing aside and laughing at the commotion. Then, Bernard suddenly gave one of his rare low laughs and held up his hands.

'Très bien, you win, Adam, you hide behind a woman, eh?'

Now we all laughed, and Adam lowered me down to the marble floor of the entrance hall. I smoothed the pleats of my dress and held out my hand to Adam, saying, 'My shoes, now!'

I sat on one of the delicate hall chairs, and Adam knelt in front of me, buckling on my shoes. As he slid my hands over my ankles, I felt a rush of love for him and remembered our promise of later. I looked up at Bernard who was looking at us. There was the remnant of laughter in his face and a definite fondness in his smile.

'Sorry, Bernard,' I said, 'Adam can't help being so ridiculous. We don't need the car tonight.'

Bernard nodded, 'I am invited to a dinner of the Carabinieri in Ancona. My friend called to ask me to join them. If you are sure?'

Adam, still kneeling, answered 'A reunion of Italian cops? Have a great time then, old man.'

Adam began to rise, and at the same time, Bernard moved forward and with an almost unnoticeable touch, sent Adam sprawling on the marble floor as he said, 'Next time this old man put you in the fountain, bien sur.'

Adam had curled up and was now laughing too much to stand.

I gave him a light kick with the toe of my sandal, 'Do get up, Adam. behave yourself.' Then I turned to Bernard, 'We'll meet for breakfast, Bernard. Have a good evening. *Bonne soirée.*'

'*Merci*, Mademoiselle, you too. Enjoy your dinner, if this ridiculous boy ever stops laughing.' He leant down and grabbed the hood of Adam's Parka and pulled him to his feet and gave him a light shake, 'I go now, young man, and leave you to care for Mademoiselle Eve.'

Adam, still trying to stop laughing, said,

'Oh, no problem about that, Bernie, I'll care for Mademoiselle very well indeed.' Adam looked past Bernard to me as he spoke and added, 'And we intend to have an early night.'

Bernard gave a small salute and went out of the Villa into the gathering darkness. The young waiter came into the hall and looked at us with some curiosity as we stood still laughing and with Adam pushing my loafers into his Parka pockets. Obviously well trained to ignore the eccentricity of guests he gave a small polite nod and began to light the candles in the wall sconces.

We all walked on through to the dining salon, regaining our composure. Johnny and Rowena walked ahead of us, arm in arm like a stately married couple. Adam and I followed hand in hand and not quite so well-behaved as I managed to discreetly pinch Adam's bottom as we sat at our table.

The meal was as refined and delicious as the evening before, and conversation flowed smoothly. We moved on from reminiscing our time together in Tuscany to plans for the next day.

'Johnny and I have planned a visit to Recanati tomorrow. I don't suppose you and Adam have time to join us?'

I looked at Rowena in surprise, 'Recanati, why Recanati in particular?' Then I smiled, 'Of course, the birthplace of the poet Leopardi.'

Johnny gave one of his very best Italian film star smiles at me, 'I'm sure you have already been to his Palazzo. We've read all your papers on Leopardi and Dante. It would be such an honour if you would accompany us.'

'Well, I did visit once. I suppose it must be more than five years ago now. I'd love to go again. What about you, Adam?'

Adam looked up from attacking the very large t-bone steak on a board in front of him, 'Me? You know me, Princess, I'm interested in everything. Leonardo, Leopardi, Leo anyone-o, whoever. As long as I have my camera, then I'm happy.'

I looked at him fondly as he returned to sawing another slice from his steak. It was true. He was always so happy.

14

The next day, directly after an early breakfast we set off for the hill town of Recanati. Bernard at the wheel, Rowena sitting comfortably beside him and in the back, Adam sitting between Johnny and me. The Mercedes was roomy enough, but I was unused to sitting somewhat squashed up to the window. Adam had insisted on sitting in the middle, and his long legs were folded up neatly. As usual, he was flicking through some photos on his iPad.

'This is the one!' He said, sounding very pleased with himself. He passed the iPad to Johnny.

'Beautiful, Adam, wonderful. A modern Madonna masterpiece.' Johnny looked dreamy and passed to the screen to me, adding, 'Rowena is so beautiful.'

I nodded in agreement and flicked the screen across to the next shot. 'I love this one, too. There's so much in the background, just like the scenery behind the Mona Lisa, in fact.'

Adam took the screen from me, 'You are a clever clogs, aren't you? That was exactly what I was going for... still, I think the closer shot is better. The light is perfect and the framing of the roses... yeah, perfect.'

I took the screen back and looked again at the background. It was of the formal gardens rolling down to the edge of the forest. I spread my thumb and finger across to enlarge the image and then gave a gasp of shock. 'Look, there's a man on the edge of the forest. I saw him the other evening but forgot to tell you about it.'

Adam leaned over and looked at the enlarged section of the photo. 'Good God, so there is... not like me to miss that. I can hardly believe it.'

'Well, he's there all right. Look Johnny.' I passed the iPad to Johnny and he, too, studied the small screen.

'Yes, you're right. There's a man bending low, running maybe?'

'Exactly. I saw him the other evening when we were at dinner. He looks rather a shady character, don't you think?'

Adam laughed, 'Shady? Come off it Princess, you sound like a girl in an Agatha Christie mystery. Look out, what ho, I say, there's a shady cove lurking in the undergrowth.' Once again Adam had attempted to copy my voice in a high falsetto. Once again I dug him hard in the ribs which was more difficult than usual as I was sitting so close to him. Johnny was laughing,

'Are you trying to sound like Eve? That was a pathetic attempt, Adam. Eve has a low sexy voice not a squeaky one like that.'

'God, you're right, of course, Johnny... she does sort of purr, doesn't she? It comes over so well on TV. Yes, you're quite right, sort of velvety and silkily sexy.'

I gave Adam a harder dig in his ribs and pushed him into Johnny.

'When you two have quite finished your puerile and sexist discussion...'

Bernard interrupted,

'We arrive at Recanati, Mademoiselle Eve. Do you want to go directly to the museum of Leopardi?'

I sat forward, ignoring the two men who were now sniggering like naughty schoolboys,

'Thank you, Bernard, yes, well as near as you can get. I seem to remember it's a pedestrian area.'

I looked out of the window as Bernard drove slowly through the narrow cobbled streets. I had only stayed a short time in the town when I was a student at Cambridge. Five years ago, maybe four? Nothing seemed to have changed, I thought, which was the joy of the historic centres of most Italian cities, towns and villages. Then the car slowed as we entered a small piazza.

'This is the nearest place, Mademoiselle Eve. Shall I leave you here?'

'That's fine, Bernard. I remember the town quite well. We'll walk from here. Will you join us at the museum?'

'Non, merci, Mademoiselle. Here I cannot stop so I take the car around and you call me when you are ready, Yes?'

'Fine, thank you, Bernard.'

Bernard turned off the engine and quickly got out and opened my door for me and then went round to open Rowena's door. I stood beside her for a moment, enjoying the sunshine. Then I said,

'Shall we walk together, Rowena? There's an interesting row of artisan shops around the corner. I need some retail therapy after a journey with the lads. I bought a lovely leather handbag here some time ago. What do you think?'

'Ooh yes, I'd love that. Maybe Johnny and Adam could wait in that café over there.' She turned to Johnny and said, 'Eve and I are going to look at some shops as we're still early for the museum appointment. Why don't you and Adam have a coffee or something.'

Johnny looked crestfallen and slightly anxious, saying, 'I'll come with you, Ro.'

'Johnny, no! Eve and I won't be more than half an hour. Go on, I shall be fine.'

Johnny kicked his hand-made shoe in the dust of the cobbled pavement and looked decidedly sulky. Suddenly he looked like the spoilt young man of the Castello that I had met in Tuscany. Adam patted Johnny on the back and said,

'Come on, Johnny, let's have a cappuccino and let the girls be bossy. We'll wait for you in that caff over there, the one called Gino's, OK?'

Rowena and I set off, arm in arm and very soon we were engrossed in shopping. I always enjoyed the individual shops that somehow survived in the small towns of Italy. I found the same leather shop that I had told Rowena about. We spent some time examining the array of brightly dyed leather bags.

'Just look at this green one, Eve. Isn't it splendid? It's like a backpack. I think it would be ideal for carrying all the baby clobber that one seems to need. What do you think?'

I held the bag for a moment, trying to imagine what a small baby needed that could fill a bag more suited to a backpacker.

'Hmm, yes, I suppose so. It's quite heavy... lovely leather, of course.'

'But so soft. Anyway, I expect Johnny will be carrying it for me. I have to have it.' Rowena held out the bag to the young man who had been sitting in the background, stitching and cutting as we browsed. He looked pleased and took the bag to wrap it. Rowena was not finished,

'And I'll take this cream suede wallet for Johnny. Can you gift wrap it please?'

I turned away to look through some clutch purses and to hide my smile. There was something very confident and determined about the quiet Rowena.

'And I'll take this tan clutch bag and this small leather box, please. I'd like the box gift wrapped, too.'

Now the dark-faced young man was smiling and nodding happily as he neatly packaged our purchases and place them in two large carrier bags.

We left the shop with that lift in spirits that follows some indulgent spending. I took both the bags in one hand, and we began to walk back toward the piazza, arm in arm.

Suddenly, there was the high-pitched noise of a scooter behind us. I turned and saw two young men riding toward us, their black helmets low down as the drew near. My instinct told me they were trouble and I stood in front of Rowena terrified that she might e hurt. Then, as they passed, I felt a hard tug on my shoulder, and my bag was suddenly flying through the air. I dropped the carrier bags and stepped forward and just caught the end of the broken strap. I yanked at it hard, so hard that the man riding pillion was pulled from his seat and the scooter lurched sideways. I moved further forward and gave a hard kick to the man now lying in the gutter and grabbed my bag back. The other man threw the scooter onto its side, the engine dying and looked at me through the dark screen of his helmet. He took one step toward me, and I raised my arm in a karate movement and stood still. He looked at me for what seemed a long moment, then grabbed the arm of his companion, and they both ran off.

I turned to Rowena who had taken shelter in the doorway of the leather shop. Soon, we were surrounded by a noisy group of people. I put my arms around Rowena,

'Are you all right, Ro, are you OK?'

To my surprise, I realised that Rowena was laughing and not crying as I had first thought.

'I'm fine. You were amazing, Eve, when you're bored with your wine series, you ought to go for a female James Bond part.'

I laughed with relief and was about to try to answer all the questions that were flying through the air at us. Yes, we were both fine, no, nothing had been stolen, no we did not blame the beautiful town of Recanati, yes, we were quite sure the scooter men were immigrants. That was something I had expected. I had spent enough time in Italy to know that any crime committed would always be laid at the feet of a gipsy or immigrant. It was just their way. I was sure they didn't really believe it, but their national pride spoke for them. I had long since tried to make any sense of it. Then, to my further relief, I saw Adam and Johnny running toward us.

15

Somehow, we had managed to get to our meeting at the Leopardi museum on time, or rather an acceptable Italian quarter of an hour late. Rowena and I had survived the barrage of questions from a bemused Adam and an almost tearful Johnny.

'Enough, both of you. Let's just enjoy our visit now.' I said, 'The Carabinieri have the scooter and will find the wretched thieves, I'm sure. Enough, it's all over.' I glared at Adam, tired of the endless questioning and repetition of the details of our attack. 'Look, I even have a new laptop bag. The young man in the shop insisted, and he's going to mend the strap on my old one. There, you see, all over, completely over.'

Rowena laughed and squeezed Johnny's arm, 'I agree, let's forget it now. Although I must say, it will be some time before I can forget seeing Eve turn into some whirling dervish.'

'That's my wife, all right. One minute she looks so delicate she could snap and the next minute she's an Amazon warrior. You know she studied martial arts, don't you? What was it, Eve? Karate?'

'No, no, I studied Taekwondo when I was a teenager, and I keep in practice, just a little. It was Bernard's idea, actually.'

'Ackchewally, I think self-defence for women is an excellent idea. Good old Bernie. Still, he won't be pleased when he hears what happened the minute you were out of his sights.'

'I really don't see why we have to tell him and do stop calling him old Bernie. You'll end up being tipped in a fountain again.'

'I know, I know, I just can't resist it. Of course, we have to tell him, the police will come back to you, and he's bound to find out.'

'I suppose so. Anyway, we can worry about that later. Looks like the museum director is heading our way. I think I remember her, actually.' I glared at Adam, 'Do not repeat me.'

'Ackchewally I wasn't going to. I was about to suggest you change from warrior mode to eminent scholar.'

The director of the museum, an elderly silver-haired, silver-voiced woman came up to me, holding out her hand in welcome.

'*Benvenuti, tutti!* How wonderful to see you again, Eve.' She spoke impeccable English and had a quiet, somewhat austere manner. I did remember her quite well now.

'*Dottoressa Faleroni, piacere.*' I shook her smooth, cool hand and thought that she seemed to have aged more than the four or five years since I had last met her. I wondered if she was thinking exactly the same about me? I introduced Rowena and Johnny as students of Leopardi, and then Adam, who was following, carrying our somewhat crumpled carrier bags.

'*Piacere, piacere*, Eve. Please, please, you must all call me Serena. I hate the use of *Professoressa*, especially as any graduate in Italy immediately snatches the title after their first degree. It means nothing here.' She smiled graciously and took Adam's hand,

'Of course, you are the celebrated Adam Wright. The war photo-journalist.' She continued to shake Adam's hand for a long while as she studied his face carefully, 'I am delighted to meet you. I went to your exhibition at the Imperial War Museum in London. Such an impressive and highly emotional exhibition.'

Adam nodded, blushing slightly under his new tan.

'Thank you, I'm sorry we didn't meet when you were there. I tried to go most days but...'

'Oh, I know you have taken on a new assignment with Eve Sinclair. We may live in a small hill town in Italy, but now, with the internet, we are abreast of all the mondial news and gossip. By the local grapevine, I already know that there was a regrettable incident just around the corner. I am so sorry your visit should begin so unpleasantly.'

I thought for a moment she was going to say the attackers were certainly not from Recanati, but Dottoressa, call-me Serena, Faleroni was a sophisticated woman and, waving her elegant hand in a way to express her despair at the ways of the modern world, she added with a shrug,

'Very sad and terrible. So many young people out of work, taking illegal substances and turning to crime to fund their addiction. Please, come into my studio and sit for a while.'

She beckoned to the young woman behind the reception counter, who jumped up and came over to us. Our carrier bags were quickly handed over, and the young woman almost bobbed a curtsey and the scuttled back to sit behind her desk.

Adam and I exchanged quick amused glances, sharing amusement at the autocratic manner of the director and then we all followed her along a wide, rather gloomy gallery, our footsteps ringing out in the heavy silence. At the very end, Serena opened double doors and ushered us into a large book-lined room. I looked around, certain that I had not met her here before. As though sensing my curiosity, Serena said,

'I have recently installed myself in this salon. I spend many hours at the Palazzo, probably more than I do in my own home, so I have made myself comfortable. The Leopardi family still live on the upper floors, so I made this room my working base. Unfortunately, I do not benefit from the fine views that the upper floor windows enjoy.' She sighed and fanned her hand in front of her face, her lips drawn down in displeasure as she added, 'The family also have a lovely rooftop belvedere.'

Then she waved her hand dismissively in the air, as though to give up in the thought and gestured that we should be seated in the elegant 18th-century chairs set around an inlaid walnut table. There was a small writing desk in the window, and a shaft of sunlight glanced through the shutters and lit part of the room, glinting on the bright coloured glass fruits hanging from each stem of the large crystal chandelier. Hmm, Murano, I thought to myself, as I took my seat and then looked down at the vibrant colours in the antique silk rugs. Yes, Serena Faleroni had made herself very comfortable indeed.

Adam, who could never be seated as easily as anyone else, roamed around the room, studying the leather bound books and then went over to the window.

'What a beautiful place to work, Serena,' he said, expressing exactly what I was thinking. 'Do you get many tourists visiting?'

Serena had taken her place in a small armchair in the middle of the group of chairs, and now she waved her hand again and wrinkled her delicate, rather aristocratic nose,

'Indeed, we do, we have our wine cellars too, of course,' She paused and gave me a cold smile and then continued, 'Often too many in the summer, but I only allow limited numbers for guided tours. If visitors haven't booked then sometimes they have to wait outside... often for an hour or more.'

I couldn't help thinking that this idea seemed to please Serena, then she continued,

'But, of course, we receive many serious scholars, and they are made very welcome. Our library, you must visit it after we have talked, has a collection of twenty thousand books or more.'

Adam raised his eyebrows in surprise, 'That's a large collection. Were they all books written by Leopardi and books he owned?'

'Well, his father, Count Monaldo, commissioned an immense collection of literary and scientific works. Then we have the family archives dating back to the year 1207, and halls devoted to the evolution of printing, ancient manuscripts and incunabula.'

'Incunabula?' Adam repeated the word and raised his eyebrows. I knew that he was about to ask for an explanation but at that moment the door opened and a young woman brought in a silver tray laden with a large jug of orange juice and five very beautiful cut glass tumblers.

I sipped my glass of chilled fresh orange juice and tried to feel sorry that Dottoressa, call-me Serena, Faleroni had to manage without a panoramic bella vista or even a rooftop belvedere.

16

'Bernard was so furious, wasn't he?' I said sleepily. I was lying in bed and waiting for Adam to join me. We had eaten another excellent dinner at the Villa, and I was pleasantly full and slightly intoxicated by the excellent wines that I had chosen to accompany it. Johnny was still as pregnant as Rowena, apparently, and not drinking alcohol. Adam only ever drank one glass, more to please me than himself and Bernard never drank alcohol on the premise that he might need to drive. So, maybe I had drunk a little more than usual. I looked up at the ornate ceiling and enjoyed the cherubs dancing with garlands of flowers. I vaguely made a mental memo to thank Melanie for her clever choice of hotel, and then Adam bounced into bed beside me.

'Yeah, so mad. I don't think I've ever seen him so angry. He stormed into that silent library like a raging bull.'

I giggled, 'I think the serene Call-me-Serena director was quite ruffled.'

Adam laughed, too, 'What a woman. Do you think she was disappointed you didn't visit the wine cellars?' Before I could reply, he added, 'So austere and autocratic. Do you think you'd have grown old like that if you hadn't met me?'

I turned to look at him, forgetting his question about the Leopardi wine cellars and answering only, 'Why ever should you think that?'

Then, realising that Adam was trying to rile me, I replied, 'Well anyway, if you hadn't met me you'd probably have turned into a camera.'

'That's a fine surreal idea. I rather like it. I sometimes wish you weren't so clever, Princess. I'm so proud of you, though. When Serena showed me they had your translation of that old poem... what was it?'

'*L'Appressamento della Morte.*'

'Sounds rather grim. Something about death?'

'Yes, The Approach of Death. It is a sad poem.'

'Why did you choose it for translation? Rather a morbid choice, surely?'

'It was in *terza rima* and heavily influenced by Petrarch and Dante.'

'Aha, your old mate Dante. Now I get it. And your own poems are in *terza rima*, aren't they? Serena had a copy of that, too. Johnny and Rowena were well impressed. Aren't you proud?'

'More amazed. I never really thought anyone would buy it. I consider it an obscure little book published by my vanity.'

'Vanity. That's a great word, isn't it? I guess you are a little vain although I'm not sure you can be, not really.'

'I no longer have any idea what you are talking about, Adam. I'm so sleepy.'

'That's because you're sloshed.'

'I am not sloshed.' I gave Adam an elbow dig in his ribs and, without his usual Parka protection, I felt him flinch.

He turned toward me, 'If you're not sloshed then tell me a story.'

'Oh no, no, no, last time you fell fast asleep while I was still talking.'

'I'm sure I didn't. Well, explain to me about *terza rima* then.'

'I've told you before, it's a rhyming pattern.'

'Yeah, I sort of remember. I did Shakespearean sonnets for A level... something rings a bell.'

He stroked my hair back from my forehead as he spoke and suddenly I was no longer drowsy. I moved quickly and sat astride him, letting my hair fall forward to brush his chest as I chanted,

'a b a b, c d c d, e f e f, g g... that's the pattern of a Shakespearean sonnet, a little song... a sonetto, diminutive of the Italian word, sound, of course.'

'Of course, my love, I'm sure I knew that. Shall I compare thee to a summer's day... so that would be the first line a.' Adam was breathing heavily now as he moved inside me.

I placed my hands on his shoulders as I continued,

'Yes, the well-loved Sonnet 18, well known because it is so perfect and simple to understand. Three quatrains, four lines of verse grouped together by a rhyme sequence, and a concluding coupling, I mean, couplet.'

'My English teacher read it to us. Even my tough old gang were silenced by the beauty of it. My favourite line is 'Rough winds do shake the darling buds of May. Ah, that's the second 'a' and such pretty imagery... you have darling buds, did I ever tell you that?' Adam's voice was husky as he reached up to cup my breasts in his hands and said, 'Go on, tell me more.'

I sighed with pleasure and said, 'Shakespeare...'

Adam interrupted me, sighing, 'I've never thought about his name before, Shake-Spear. Great name when you think about it. Don't stop, tell me more.'

'Shakespeare, yes, an ancient Norman name, used in Britain after the 1066 Conquest. A name given to a confrontational man, derived from the Old English schakken, meaning to brandish, and spear... well, oh, ohh, meaning spear.'

'A better name than I thought... oh, schakk, yes, I love all those old words with k in them.' Adam almost groaned as he added, 'How I love to schakk you, my beautiful Princess.'

I stretched up and threw my hair back over my shoulders as I continued slowly,

'Did you learn about his introduction of the iambic pentameter? The repeated pattern of stressed and unstressed syllables.'

'Silly balls... now there's a word...'

'Are you concentrating?'

'Oh yes, yes, definitely. What was that about panting metres?'

'Penta is Greek for five, of course, five repeated patterns. Stressed followed by unstressed.'

'Of course, yeah, I knew that, So long lives this and this gives life to thee.'

Adam moved in the rhythm of each alternate word, and I struggled to answer as he murmured,

'More, tell me more sonnety stuff.'

'The Petrarchan sonnet, oh, ohhh, sometimes called the Italian sonnet, has a different rhyme scheme. The first eight lines are the octet and the following six lines, a sestet.'

Adam pushed slowly deeper and deeper inside me as he murmured, 'A sextet?'

I chanted slowly, 'a b b a, a b b a, c d e c d e... do you see the difference?'

'More, more, tell me again and again, my love.'

'An example then? 'Upon the breeze, she spread her golden hair'. Petrarch's famous sonnet 90, of course.'

'Of course, I'm sure I knew that, too.' Adam murmured, 'But is that your terza rima?'

'No, no. I forgot that's what I was telling you about. I'm losing the thread of my lecture.' I exhaled slowly, feeling my muscles contract and then continued slowly, 'Terza rima has a three-line stanza, like links in a chain, a b a b c b c d c d e d.'

Adam moved his hands down to my hips, and I strove to hold onto my explanation, adding in a breathless murmur,

'But there is no limit to the number of lines… oh, oh… although the end is either a single line or, as I prefer to use in my own… oh, ohhh… work, a couplet repeating and rhyming with the middle line of the final… aahhh… the final tercet.'

Then, my poetry lesson blazoned, flared and flowered to an end, and I fell forward on top of Adam.

17

Breakfast the next morning began as a very subdued affair. Bernard had not recovered his usual good humour by any means and sat silently sipping his small black coffee, occasionally glowering at Adam. Johnny and Adam exchanged the odd word but were both hungrily eating large omelettes. Rowena was the only one attempting to lighten the atmosphere. I took my metaphorical hat off to her.

'Another splendid day,' she said cheerily in between sips of her frothy hot chocolate. 'Haven't we been lucky with the weather?'

I murmured something about the early Autumn when the weather could change quickly, something so humdrum that I felt ashamed of my lack of effort. Somehow, Rowena, so pregnant and vulnerable, had survived the previous day's event better than any of us. Then, she said,

'You know, Eve, we forgot our shopping. It must still be with the receptionist at the museum. We'll have to go back and pick it up today sometime.'

Before I could reply, Bernard almost rose to his feet and said in a quiet but somehow forceful voice,

'Non, non, non. This is not what is happening. *Excusez-moi*, Madame Rowena, but now I must talk.'

We all stopped eating and drinking, Adam actually held his forkful of omelette in suspension, half-way to his open mouth. Then Bernard continued, 'Today I make the plans. Soon...'

But he was interrupted by the sound of Adam's phone ringing. Adam lowered his fork to his plate and hastily answered the call and then, still listening to the voice on the other end, he looked at Bernard in alarm. Now we were all looking at Adam, waiting for him to explain why he seemed so concerned. Bernard sat back in his seat and tipped down the last of his coffee and returned to looking like the personification of a thundercloud.

Adam clicked off his phone and said, 'That was Lucinda, she said we should look on YouTube as...'

Then, Adam, in turn, was interrupted by my phone ringing. I scrambled in my new bag, not yet used to the many interior compartments so it rang off before I could catch it. I looked at the last caller and saw it had been Melanie.

'That was Melanie Powers. I'll call her after breakfast.' I said, but then it rang again. How is it that the second time a caller rings it manages to sound louder and more urgent? This time I caught it,

'Melanie, sorry I missed you, just now. How are you?'

Then the storm that had been brewing over our quiet breakfast erupted into a confusion of phone calls and text messages. Only Rowena remained calm as she quietly continued to sip her hot chocolate.

Even when Adam found the Youtube video of our attack in the narrow street of Recanati, she only smiled gently as though with a pleasant reminiscence.

The short video began just as I raised my hand and caught the strap of my bag. Obviously taken on someone's phone, the action was jagged with the hand-held movement, but it was clear enough to show my face, my hair flying around in the air as I circled and landed a good kick just under the helmet of the attacker. He jerked back, clutching his throat with a black-gloved hand. The camera followed me closely as I grabbed my bag and then turned to Rowena who was huddled in the doorway of the leather shop, her arms around her swollen belly. When the screen returned to the small arrow to replay, I saw that my name was in the title 'Eve Sinclair fights back'.

Then, we all looked at each other in silence before Adam clicked on the arrow, skipped the ad of some wordy website builder, and played it through again. This time I strained to see through the dark glass of the helmet of the man that I kicked, but there was only a glint of his eyes, nothing recognisable. As the scooter fell on its side, wheels still spinning, there was, at least, an identifiable shot of the registration plate. I looked across the table to Bernard who was on his phone, his dark eyebrows drawn into a straight line as he looked down at the table, ignoring me. Johnny, also on the phone, was nodding and already had tears caught in his long dark eyelashes as he spoke in Italian. Adam was mesmerised, looking again at the video. Rowena carefully put her cup down in the saucer and then reached over and patted my hand.

'You were amazing, Eve. Extraordinary. Thank you for saving me.'

'Oh no, not at all. I should probably have let the wretched man take my bag. I just reacted automatically. I think I was angry at the thought of losing everything in my bag, you know, personal stuff and especially my notes.'

'Well, I think you were like superwoman, and I shall definitely take a course in self-defence when I've had my baby. Probably not the time for it right now.' She gave a small giggle and patted her stomach.

'How do you stay so calm, Rowena? I admire that so much.'

'Calm? Well, yes, I suppose I am. Just before I met Johnny, I spent nearly a year in India studying yoga. Like your father, I went into a retreat. I meditate once or twice a day, with Johnny now. I think it has helped him face old demons. Find himself, as they say.'

She laughed again as if it was all of little consequence. I wanted to know more, especially as she had mentioned my father but it was not the right time. The air was full of electronic beeps, and ringtones and we were all caught in the eye of the storm.

18

More than anything, it was a media storm that caught us all in its grip. I think we all knew it was time to listen to Bernard and take his advice. So, as he set off for Recanati to retrieve our shopping and meet the local police, we all sat obediently on the terrace of the Villa.'

'We're grounded.' said Adam, 'Can't even go down to the sea.'

'Better not,' agreed Johnny, 'Bernard said to stay in the grounds of the villa.'

'Well, it's hardly a punishment, is it?' Rowena said in a cheery voice. 'It's so beautiful here, and Bernard said he'd be back in time to take you to your meeting at the vineyard, Eve.'

'True,' I yawned and stretched out on the cushioned sun-lounger, 'I think we all need a rest.'

'I hate rest. I mean what does it mean? Sleep is one thing but rest?' Adam, unable to relax, was striding around the terrace, looking longingly at the blue line of the horizon.'What was it you said about seeing a man down there by the edge of the forest, Eve? I think I just saw someone moving around.'

I sat up and looked to where he was now pointing the zoom lens of his camera.

'Yes, down there, just on the edge of the trees, but I can't see anything now.'

'I think I'll go down and take a look-see and...'

To my surprise, Rowena interrupted Adam, her voice as quiet as usual but much more determined,

'You will do no such thing, Adam Wright. What are you thinking? Bernard told us to stay right here, and that's what you should do.'

Adam looked at Rowena in surprise and then gave one of his usual lop-sided grins,

'You're right, of course, Ro. I wasn't thinking. I have a dreadful hatred of being told what to do. But you're quite right, and Bernie gave me a good dressing down about leaving Eve and you to go off shopping alone. Apparently, I deserted my duty as stand-in bodyguard. Though honestly, I think Eve has proved she is quite able to look after herself. Still..'

He faltered to a halt and looked longingly down across the formal villa gardens to the stretch of woodland that led to the seashore.

Johnny, who was stretched out in perfect comfort on a sun lounger close to Rowena's, raised his dark glasses and said,

'Give it a break, Adam, just relax for an hour or so, can't you. After all, Bernard told us about the risk of kidnap throughout Eve's childhood and how he had dreaded it... for God's sake, man, why do you and Eve both go looking for trouble?'

I sat up, for some reason feeling I should go to Adam's defence, especially as he had awarded me his confidence in my own ability. I spoke strictly at Johnny,

'We don't look for trouble, it just seems to find us. Remember the mess we ended up in at your Castello in Tuscany? Your family would be in a dreadful state if we hadn't been there.'

'True, OK, I give you that.' Johnny waved his arms in the air as if to surrender and then added, 'My weird family have always been in some mess or another, but I have to admit you saved us from ourselves.'

Now I felt embarrassed at reminding him of his dysfunctional family, and so I changed the drift of the subject,

'I can't believe that Bernard and my father were so concerned about the risk of my being kidnapped as a child. But now I do remember that one of my school friends was abducted and finally found alive but in a poor way on some Greek island.'

Adam turned back from his inspection of the view through his zoom lens, 'It's a dreadful thought, isn't it, living with that sort of fear. Do you think when your Pa lost all his money that he felt some sort of relief?'

I couldn't think how to answer, so I tried for another change of subject.

'Anyway, Melanie is thrilled by the whole thing. Can you imagine how she will use yesterday's attack for publicity? There's nothing I can do to calm her down, and it's already all out there anyway. She'll have a field day.'

Adam sighed, 'She will indeed. The price of money and celebrity are probably about even stevens.'

He laughed then and threw himself down on the sun lounger next to mine, 'That's a deep philosophical thought for me, isn't it? Now, while I'm suffering rest, Johnny, listen up and stop gazing in wonder at Rowena for one minute... can I ask you and Rowena a favour?'

Rowena smiled sweetly, 'Anything we can possibly do, Adam, anything.'

I smiled at the thought that Rowena certainly made all the decisions now in Johnny's life and then Adam added,

'Would you and Johnny join us on our visit to the vineyard? There's someone I'd like you to meet.'

Johnny looked at Rowena for confirmation, and as she smiled and nodded at him, he said happily, 'Be delighted, cool!'

'Exactly,' Adam smiled and closed his eyes as he rested his head back on the cushion, 'Yeah, cool.'

19

Bernard had returned to the Villa at exactly eleven-thirty as he had promised and we were all ready to leave for the vineyard. He seemed surprised but pleased that Rowena and Johnny were joining us. He held open the front passenger door for Rowena and carefully adjusted the rake of the seat and settled her comfortably. I sat again behind Bernard and Adam took his place in the middle, between me and Johnny. There was still some awkward silence, and I think we were all waiting for Bernard to tell us about his morning.

He drew slowly away from the Villa at his usual steady speed. As we passed through the high iron entrance gates, Adam craned forward to look out my side window. I knew he was trying to see along the edge of the wood, but I gave him a quick dig in the ribs to silence him, knowing this was not the time to speak about anything or particularly anyone strange that we had noticed. I put my fingers to my lips and frowned at Adam, and he nodded. Unfortunately, Bernard had caught my conspiratorial dumb show.

'So,' he said, almost exploding with rage, 'Now what are you two planning about?' He pulled the car into a small sandy lay-by at the side of the road and switched off the engine. He turned full around and looked at Adam directly, 'So, tell me, what is Mademoiselle Eve warning you not to say?'

'Oh, nothing, nothing really.' Adam tried to look casual and began to adjust the lens on his camera.

'You are very bad liar, Adam. Very bad. Now, first, you listen to me. I have spent some time in Recanati sorting your mess. My friend comes from the Carabinieri in Ancona, and all is now fixed. The two men arrested and held on charges of assault. Many witnesses already and you and Rowena do not have to appear in court but your statements to be read. Also, the homes of the men are searched and a stack of drugs found. This matter is now finished for us. I collect the bag forgotten by you all except Mademoiselle Rowena. It is now in the boot. That, later. I collect your repaired bag from the shop, that, also in the boot, also later. Then, I speak to the *Dottoressa* at the Palazzo Leopardi and find she is responsible for placing this video on YouTube. She wants publicity for her museum, bien sur. Now, the local paper has big article planned on your visit. Also, I speak to Melanie Powers, and she tell me there will be much media interest. Then, I speak to Miss Lucinda to find out how it is in London and she tell me is in the national paper already this morning. Then your father, Mademoiselle Eve, he was...'

I interrupted, having heard just about enough, but shocked to know he had spoken with my normally distant and elusive father. 'My father is still in London?'

'*Mais oui*, he is with Miss Lucinda when I call her. He thinks, like me, the situation is not at all good.

Like me, he says to be very careful. We speak later about what you not tell me. All later. *Alors*, now, I drive, and you think about it all.'

He turned around and before I could say another word, he turned on the engine and pulled out of the lay-by, and resumed his silence.

I looked at his reflection in the driving mirror, but he didn't catch my glance as he would have done normally. I accepted that I was still in disgrace. Adam gave me a gentle nudge in my ribs and said,

'Do you want a butterscotch, Princess?' I nodded, and Adam passed the bag around. Only Bernard refused to take a sweet.

Then, talking with her mouthful of butterscotch, Rowena said,

'I think we should all do exactly as Bernard says. He is absolutely right.'

We all agreed hastily, mumbling with our mouths full of buttery sweetness.

We arrived at the Casa Verde promptly at noon and as soon as Bernard turned off the engine the farmhouse door opened and a middle-aged man, wearing a Nike track suit, gold trainers and a black baseball cap came out to greet us.

'Benvenuti, benvenuti a tutti!' He glanced at Rowena and then turned to me. 'Welcome, *Signora Eve Sinclair, un gran piacere!*'

I shook his hand, trying not to wince at his vice-like grasp and then made an explanation for our group being larger than invited. Signor Marioni seemed delighted to have more visitors than expected and ushered us into the farmhouse, taking Rowena's arm and paying her extra attention.

Bernard waited by the car, and I glanced back to him before I went into the darkness of the farmhouse hall. He raised his hand to me and nodded, not quite a smile, but at least his brow was clear of his frown. I gave a sigh of relief, hoping that we were nearly back in his good books. I had plenty of work ahead of me and needed to think about wine, not hooligans and kidnapping.

We were invited to sit around the long scrubbed table in the room that led off the hall. The sun filtered through the ancient narrow windows and lit upon the copper pans and an impressive array of silver cups and shields. Apart from a glass case of stuffed animals, obviously hunting trophies, I decided it was a very pleasant room... maybe worth a photo.

Then I heard Adam asking if Signor Marioni would permit him to take a photo... as so often, reading my mind. But Signor Marioni threw his large hands in the air dramatically,

'*No, no, no, per favore*! No here. Here is all old style, later I show you my new house. My wife is there now. I build a magnificent house with the large swimming pool, you see later.'

My heart sank as I imagined the lavish Californian style property that I would be expected to admire. Most probably a concrete blot on an idyllic hilltop. I was not new to this game, and I decided to speak up quickly,

'Thank you, Signor Marioni, but maybe another time. Today I would love to visit your cellars and taste your wines. Your son, Luigi, gave me some information but...'

'Luigi, my son, he knows little.' Signor Marioni gave a dismissive shrug and pulled a rather unkind face of disapproval.

Adam entered the conversation, 'Is Luigi here today? He gave us a good tour of your estate when you were away the other day.'

I looked at Adam in surprise as he had not strictly told the truth. As I recalled, Luigi had not even bothered to walk down through the vines with us. Signor Marioni seemed equally surprised as he said,

'*Si, si*, my son is now having coffee.' He tapped his wristwatch, and I noticed it was a clumpy, very bright gold affair, 'Is his normal time for the breakfast. Is fault of his mother, certain for sure. Always I say her, is not good. *Prego, prego... non viziare nostro figlio.'*

There was another shrug of his broad shoulders and this time he slammed his fist down on the broad planks of the table, 'La mamma è sempre la mamma...' There was another slam on the table, causing the glasses set ready for our tasting to wobble, *'Ma, ma... il mammismo? No? Luigi, il mio figlio... come il ricco ragazzo viziato'* He turned to Adam as though for male support as he ranted on, *'Se non assaggia il bastone, la vizi. No? Non e vero?'*

Adam raised his eyebrows and looked to me. I bit my lip and then muttered a short translation,

'Spare the rod, spoil the child. I think Signor Marioni regards his son as a mother's boy.'

Adam nodded and was about to reply, but then Signor Marioni stood up and began to pour wine into the glasses on the table. He seemed to have entirely forgotten his angry outburst and turned to me with a quick smile, baring all his very white teeth and one gold one.

'Skin off your teeth, Signora Eve.' His toast, as he raised his glass, was inappropriate and appropriate at the same time. I raised my glass and replied with a feeble,

'Cin, cin!'

Adam, came to my rescue saying, 'Have you spent time in the States, Signor Marioni.'

'Yes, yes, one year we live in California. My wife is from there. Her family also making wine in

Napa Valley.' He pulled another of his grimaces, 'American Mediterranean style, so many grape *varietà,* French, Italian, Spanish... hybrid...' Now he knocked back the contents of his glass and smacked his lips with satisfaction. 'Here, we grow Verdicchio, the finest grape in the world.' He now slapped his chest in self-congratulation.

I was beginning to heartily dislike Signor Marioni, but I had taken my first and then second sip of his pale straw-coloured chilled wine. He was right to be proud of his wine if not his son, Luigi.

I closed my eyes to intensify the senses of my palate. Fresh and fruity, medium weight, wonderful zingy acidity and yet, yes, distinctly aromatic... soft herbs, almond, a slight citrus note and with an incredibly long finish.

Or, in one word, divine. Or, a shorter word, cool.

21

'So where did you disappear to when I went through the vineyards with Signor Marioni?' I spoke quietly to Adam as we sat close together again in the back seat of the Mercedes. The atmosphere in the car had lifted to almost normal good humour, and I didn't want to let Bernard think that Adam had disappeared off. For some reason, Bernard seemed to be more angry with Adam than any of us. Did he really expect Adam to take on the role of bodyguard when Bernard was not there himself? I sighed as I thought of how closely Bernard had followed up and down the lines of vines as Signor Marioni gave me a guided tour of nearly every precious grape. Did Bernard really expect another mugger to spring out from between the leafy vines?

Adam answered quietly, 'Johnny and I went to find Luigi.'

'Did you? I thought you stayed in the farmhouse with Rowena. Why did you...' I stopped abruptly and glanced anxiously at the driving mirror to see if Bernard had heard us. Rowena was chatting to Bernard, asking questions about his wife, Elaine, and so I continued very quietly, 'I know what you're up to, Adam. You're on one of your crusades, aren't you?'

Adam looked down at his iPad and began to scroll through some photos. Recognising this as a familiar trait when he wanted to dodge a question, I reached out and clicked the screen closed. Giving him a sharp prod with my elbow, my equally familiar response, I continued again, 'Why do you go round the world thinking you can save it? What business is it of yours if Luigi is on drugs and wasting his rich life? I can never understand why you do it?'

Adam shifted away from me a little and replied in a slightly louder voice, 'And I can never understand why you don't understand, let alone ever try and help anyone.'

His harsh words infuriated and shamed me in equal measures. I could tell we were about to plummet into one of our rows. I glanced again at the driving mirror and saw that Bernard was now looking at me, his eyebrows meeting in a straight line above his dark eyes. I gave a heavy sigh and looked away from Adam and out the window. The Marchigiana landscape spread out before me in all its pastoral glory, and I sighed again.

Adam moved close to me again, 'Do you know, Princess Don't-Call-Me Princess, that you have a large vocabulary of sighs?'

I made no answer, stifling another sigh and continued to gaze at the gently rolling hills and the blue mountains in the far distance. Adam continued,

'I know at least five, maybe six. First and most frequent is the sharp exhale of breath that is exasperation, mostly in response to something I said or did. Then, there is the Princessy sigh of boredom, that can be dangerous as it precedes your lack of sympathy in anyone less clever than yourself... meaning everyone, of course. Then there is the long sigh of relief, either when you have got away with something or can escape further annoyance or boredom. You do that a lot, too. Oh yes, there is the Master of Wine sigh, when you find a wine you like... soft and appreciative but not as long and drawn out as my favourite sigh, your sweet sigh of pleasure... like now as you look at a beautiful landscape or a work of art and... well, at other times, too.'

I turned to Adam and reached up to run my fingers through his hair and then kissed him full on his slightly open mouth, to stop him from saying more and, well, because I couldn't resist.

Then, Johnny clapped his hands and said, 'Hey, hey, you two, enough, suffis e basta... I'm feeling in the way.'

Now everyone laughed, including me, and the final strands of Bernard's anger disintegrated into the Mercedes interior.

22

I awoke, on what was to be nearly our last day at the Villa, to find an empty space beside me in the bed. I was about to sigh, but remembering Adam's account of my range of sighs, I turned it into a yawn. I curled up in the bed, nestling my head into Adam's pillow, enjoying the slight remnant of his perfume. Then, I couldn't resist a tiny sigh and decided that it was of contentment. Had Adam included that in his list? And what of yawns? Tiredness or boredom? I sleepily allowed my thoughts to wander around the idea. I certainly wasn't bored and should not be tired.

After a long dinner at the Villa, once again shared with Rowena and Johnny, we had retired to bed before midnight. Bernard had excused himself from dining with us and driven into Ancona again, warning us to stay in the Villa. I wondered, idly, whether he had spent the evening with his Carabinieri comrades. I had a niggling suspicion that he was still ferreting for information about the young men who had attacked Rowena and me. I stifled another sigh at the thought and turned over in the bed and stared up at the ceiling. There the cherubs still frolicked, trailing their garlands of flowers as they flew toward each other on wings delicately touched with gold leaf. I reflected on the idea that life in the 17th century had not been all idyllic. There had still been young men wielding knives if not wearing shiny black full-face helmets. I thought then about Rowena and her calmness. How quickly she had recovered from the shock of the attack. Was she in some cocoon-like state of pregnancy or was she always so serene and confident? How would I be when, if, I became pregnant? The thought made me sit up in bed. I stretched and pushed my hair back over my shoulders and then looked down at my skinny flat stomach. I knew that Adam was quietly ready for us to begin a family but, after a few tentative discussions, he had let the matter drop. I knew very well that I was not ready. Not yet. I got up slowly and went over to the window and threw open the shutters. To my surprise, it was a grey day. Low clouds were rolling in over the distant line of the sea. A sea no longer azure blue but a soft grey only a shade greener than the sky. So, the early Autumn weather had changed quickly, just as I had mentioned to Rowena some days ago. I shivered and closed the window. Time for breakfast before finishing off my work here. I looked down to the gardens below, thinking I might see Adam. The thin glass pane had the imperfection of antiquity, and the view was slightly distorted. I traced watery bubble shape with my forefinger and then started with a small scream as the bedroom door flew open.

'You're up at last.' Adam came in on a rush of cold air, smiling and rosy-cheeked with health. I was jolted out of my reflective mood as he threw his arms around me and added, 'You've been off in one of your Eve-reveries, haven't you? I can tell by the sweet, dreamy look on your face.'

'Your hands are like ice, Adam. Let me go.'

'Sorry, but how can I when you stand there like a little nymph in your silky little nightie thingy?'

I wriggled away from him and ran into the shower and turned on the hot tap. 'Oh no you don't. I'm sure I'm late for breakfast, and I'm starving.' I locked the bathroom door and called out, 'And no picking the lock today.'

'Shame on you, Princess. As if I would do such a thing. Anyway, you are very, very late for breakfast and the staff probably want their lunch by now. Chop, chop.'

His voice was muffled by the sound of the running water and the thickness of the door. I smiled as I let the jet of hot water run over me. What was it Adam had said the other evening in the garden? Later, there was always later.

23

We were very late for breakfast. It was almost eleven o'clock when we sat down at a small table for two, set in the window. The staff were as charming and attentive as ever, and very soon I was sipping my orange juice and nibbling on a hot croissant.

'Did you tell Melanie how good this place is?' Adam looked up from his plate of fried eggs and ham. 'I think it has to be one of the best places we've ever stayed. Somehow there is no sign of management but everything runs like clockwork and nothing seems to be too much trouble. They're even laundering my Parka today.'

I looked at Adam in surprise as I knew from past adventures that his Parka had to be in a dire state before he allowed anyone to wash it.

'What have you been up to now, Adam?'

He dropped his head and attacked his eggs and, whilst I couldn't help admiring his dark blonde locks, I also knew he was evading an answer.

'Go on, tell me the worst. What happened? Adam, tell me or I shall sulk all day.'

Adam looked up, and his light blue eyes shone straight to my heart. Was he a Botticelli Jesus or a filmic Superstar? I smothered a sigh. Was it one that Adam had forgotten to describe? A sigh of pure desire.

Then, with his usual lop-sided grin, he said, 'I think I know how I could stop you from sulking, my love. But anyway, there's nothing to tell. I went for an early run down to the coast and coming back up, I slipped and fell into the undergrowth. That's all.' He put down his knife and fork and held his hands out in an act of simplicity.

'You're a terrible liar, Adam. Now, tell me the rest of the story... you were running and...'

'Well, if you must know, I went off the track a bit as I thought I'd go to where we saw that man lurking on the edge of the woods. It's deceptive, the trees are much denser than they look from here. Anyway, I kept going and came to a sort of hidden entrance with a chain across it. There's a small road, you can't see it from here, not even a road, really, just a bumpy track.'

'But how did you fall?'

'Well, I didn't really fall... I had to throw myself down on the ground.'

'What on earth...'

'Don't interrupt if you want to know the end of the story. Quite funny...'

'I'm not interrupting,' I said although I patently was, 'What do you mean, funny?'

'Well, this bloomin' huge Rottweiler suddenly leapt out of nowhere and pinned me down.'

'Oh my God, no!'

'Oh, it was OK, the dog was just doing his guard dog thing. Lovely old dog, really when you get to know him.'

'Oh no, you did your dog whispering act, didn't you? Adam, you could have been bitten, killed even. Those dogs are killers.'

'Rubbish, it's the people that train them who are to blame. Anyway, turned out this dog was a pussycat. He liked butterscotch, too.'

Now, I had to sigh. Not sure myself if it was in relief or exasperation or... amazement?

'Don't tell, Bernie, will you, Princess.' Adam resumed cutting up the large slice of ham that remained on his plate. 'I'm only just back in his favour, and I don't want another lecture in French and English on my dereliction of duty as your husband.'

'Bernard was just upset. He's fine again now. Where is he, by the way?'

'Out polishing his limo and waiting for your royal commands as usual.'

'Oh dear, I did oversleep today, didn't I?'

'Why not? You work so hard most of the time, especially when we're in London.'

I looked at Adam in surprise. It was not often that I was told that I worked hard.

'Really, do you think so? That's a compliment coming from you. You never stop. Where are Rowena and Johnny?'

Adam looked down at his plate again, and I knew there was another confession on its way.

'Well, don't get mad, Princess but yesterday they arranged to meet Luigi in Recanati.'

I was silent for a minute and then said, 'Luigi Marioni? What have you been up to now, Adam, saving a soul again? You're like some one-man band Salvation Army.'

'No, no, it was almost Johnny's idea, honestly. Yesterday, they had coffee together. I felt quite left out of it when the two of them started talking. Very similar types, handsome playboys. Anyway, Johnny was quite brilliant. He went straight to the point and told Luigi that he had been in exactly the same dark place... and your old school friend.'

'You mean, Lucinda?' My brain was struggling to piece together Adam's words.

'No, well, yes, we did get on to Luc, but I meant Johnny's sister and the state she was in until she went into rehab.'

'Oh, you mean, Lottie Harrington.' My mind raced back to our time in Tuscany, but Adam continued,

'Yeah, Johnny was amazing. Kind and yet quite firm, backed up by the sweet Rowena, of course. She came up with the idea of a trip to the Leopardi place today. That's where they've all gone. Apparently, Ro found out there was some lecture on, and it seemed a good start. But it was Johnny who suggested that Luigi should come over to stay with them in Cambridge and get his act together.'

'Stay with them in Cambridge? Goodness, is that a good idea?'

'Turns out that Luigi dropped out of Harvard, no less.'

'Really, what a shame. So what was he reading at Harvard?'

'Literature... just up your street, Eve. Anyway, Johnny told Luigi how your colleague, Lily, gave private tuition and Luigi seemed to wake up. Maybe it was the coffee kicking in, but there was that look in his eye. You know what I mean, Eve? I guess it's hope and all to do with someone caring about you. You know, giving a damn.'

I did know what he meant as we had talked before about needing someone to believe in you and seeing something of value. But was Johnny Harrington, even now in his new life with the grounded Rowena, was Johnny up to the task of rehabilitating Luigi? I felt unsure how to reply to all this information, but then I said slowly,

'I do think his father, skilful as he is as a winemaker, is something of a pig.'

'Too right. I met Signora Marioni, too. Just briefly, but long enough to recognise a woman not in love with her husband if ever I saw one. Quiet woman, somehow in control of her feelings, very uptight but well groomed in that Californian way. Not typical of the easy-going American women I've met.'

I wondered, just for a brief moment, how many easy-going American women Adam had met and how well he had known them. Then, with another repressed sigh, I tried to stay on the subject matter.

'So, does Signora Marioni spoil Luigi, as Signor Marioni so loudly complained?'

'Oh yes, I'd say so. She obviously adores her son. Kept ruffling his hair, you know, a bit much, really, a bit creepy. But then what do I know about mother love? Bernie doesn't even think I'm a good husband.'

'Rubbish, Adam. That's all blown over. Bernard knows quite well you have risked your life for me more than once on our travels. Anyway, I think you perform your husbandly duties extremely well.'
Adam looked up at me, then and I was pleased to see that my words had caused his blue eyes to deepen. So, I continued, 'Maybe you could tell Bernard that I'm going to stay all day at the Villa. I need to collate my notes... and we could go through your photos and...'
Adam stood up and grinned, 'Is that like an invitation to see your etchings? Just give me a moment. I'll find Bernard and see you in our room in a minute then.
Yes, there was always a later. Sometimes it just came a little sooner than later.

But, as it happened, our later became much later. Just as we approached the lift to go to our room, Adam's mobile buzzed. HIs ringtone was the annoying sound of a small dog yapping, and right now, as he removed his hand from massaging the back of my neck, I found it exasperating.

'Leave it Adam, read it later.'

'Ah, that magic word, later. No, better take it, it's Bernie.

I stifled a sigh, I was getting good at that, and waited to press the button to summon the lift.

Adam read the message and then frowned. I was standing close enough to see the delightful wrinkle form between his blonde eyebrows. Somehow, even his frown was enchantingly sweet, and I resisted the desire to lick his troubled brow. So much repression and not even the relief of a wistful out-breath. Wistful restraint... was that number six in my catalogue of sighs? Then, Adam clicked his phone to call Bernard.

I stepped away a pace and waited, now feeling rather cross with Adam, certain it was something that could have waited.

'Hi, Bernie. I got your message but wanted to be clear.' Adam spoke quietly into the phone, looking over his shoulder to see if we were being overheard. Now, I became interested and stood so close to Adam that I could eavesdrop on the conversation. The long hallway of the Villa was quite empty, the staff being discreetly out of sight as usual. Then I heard Bernard's voice,

'Is not good. I have the gates now closed by the Villa gardener but...'

'Are there many reporters then?' Adam asked.

'Too many. I think, *peutêtre*, ten, maybe more. I drove through with difficulty. Now I am parked on the road above the Villa. Maybe I return?'

'No, don't worry, Bernie. I can handle this, I promise. We won't take any walks in the garden on a day like this, no problem. Most celebrity paps use either the 24-70 f/2.8L or the 16-35 f2.8L so we'll keep out of range. It's been a bit like that since our wedding, and this latest is their hot celebrity news.'

'I not understand you, Adam. I think is terrible. *Ils sont charognards, comme les vautours.*'

'Well, I don't understand you either, Bernie old man, but leave it to me. I can handle this, I promise you.'

'Hmm,'

Bernard made a sound that was as doubtful as it was French. I waited silently, slightly amused at the mish-mash of their language differences.

'Anyway, Bernie,' Adam added, 'I thought you said you'd take the morning off. Go on, call your wife or something, take a coffee.'

'Adam,' Now there was no doubt in Bernard's voice, and he was beginning to sound angry again. 'You must be serious. I speak last night to Eve's father, and he is troubled. I am responsible for the safety of Eve while I am working with you both.

Now, I go to Recanati to speak again to the local Carabinieri. When I am back in France, at home with Elaine, then, and only then, I take the time off. You understand?'

'OK, Bernie. Sorry, you're quite right as usual. We won't be going out. The light is hopeless for photos today and Eve wants to write up her notes. She will be safe as houses with me here at the Villa.'

'Safehouses? What you say now?'

I could stand it no longer, so I grabbed Adam's phone and took over.

'*Allo, Bernard, c'est moi. S'il te plait ne t'inquiète pas.* Please do not worry. I shall stay in our suite here at the Villa. *Je veux rassembler mes notes.*' I turned to Adam, who was now delightfully frowning again, and I added for his benefit. 'I intend to collate my notes.'

Then, deciding quite enough time had been wasted on the subject, I cut Bernard off and pressed the elevator button. As the doors slid open, I stepped forward, but Adam took a step back.

'Won't be long. Princess, I promise. I'm just going to run down to the gates to sort this out. I'll be back before you know it... just a little bit later and I'll help you collate your pretty notes.'

Before I could answer or object he ran off down the long hallway, his Parka flying out behind him like a 17th-century cloak. I pressed the button for our floor and allowed myself a long sigh that probably registered every one of the emotions in my sigh catalogue.

Still feeling cross with Adam at his sudden decision to desert me and go down to the gates, I made my way from the lift to our room. The long corridor on this upper floor was thickly carpeted, and I moved silently along, enjoying the peace and suddenly felt quite happy to be alone for a while. Marriage, I decided, was a wonderful but very demanding way of life.

There was a long arched window at the end of the corridor, and I passed our room and went to it. The perfect architectural symmetry of the Villa centred on this corridor, and there was a commanding view across the gardens and to the horizon of the sea. The day had not brightened, and the dark green leaves of the orange trees that lined the central drive were ruffled by a light wind. I could see Adam down at the gates, now half-open, surrounded by a crowd of journalists. Was it worth a sigh, I wondered? I decided on a shrug of exasperation instead. Adam was irrepressibly Adam and behaved exactly as he thought he should. Maybe, when we had been married longer, I would begin to understand him. Yes, it was all wonderful but demanding. Even from this distance, I could see that Adam held the small crowd in his thrall. Vultures, scavengers, Bernard had called the reporters, but I had decided not to do a direct translation to Adam. He had worked as a photojournalist himself, of course. Thinking about this, I let my gaze wander over to the forest. From this higher level, I could see that there was a low flat-roofed building set in a clearing. Perhaps this was where Adam had encountered the Rottweiler? Then, as I thought about that, unable to resist a smile at the thought of Adam making easy friends with the savage guard dog, I saw a flash of light. It seemed to have come from the side of the building. I strained my eyes to see the outline of the roof and walls, but there was now no further sign of light or any movement. Had I imagined it? The day was grey and overcast but no sign of a storm or lightning. I stayed for a few minutes still staring at the building, but nothing happened. Eventually, I gave up and looked back to the gates.

Now there was a flurry of activity, the reporters turning away and moving quickly to their cars. Adam raised a hand in friendly farewell and then moved back inside the gates and closed them behind him. He looked up at the Villa and seemed to be looking directly at me. I raised my hand although I knew it was impossible for him to see me in the darkness of the window. Then, he took his camera from the pocket of his Parka and took a photo. Hadn't he told Bernard that the daylight was too poor for photography? I watched as he strode back up the drive, straight toward me, only stopping once to examine a ripening orange on one of the trees. Then, I turned away, suddenly keen to be back in our room before he reached it. Surely it was now time for our later?

'That was a later worth waiting for, Princess. I've never been jumped on by a stark naked woman before.'

I laughed, but it sounded more like a silly giggle. I was getting seriously good at having fun. I had led a sober, rather solemn life until I met Adam, but fortunately, I had always been a quick learner. When I saw Adam returning to the Villa, I had dashed back to our suite, stripped off every stitch of my clothing and hidden behind the door. As he came in, I had jumped onto his back and, with my legs firmly gripped around his waist, somehow ridden him forward until he fell on the bed. He began to laugh, and I took advantage of his helplessness and began to pull off his Parka and then every stitch of his clothing. Soon we were both tangled in a love knot and rolling over and over in the huge bed. This was fun, this was pleasure, this was how later became now, now, now.

Finally, as we lay side by side, exhausted by laughing and loving, Adam spoke first,

'You're getting very good at having fun, Princess.'

I remained silent for a moment wondering how he managed to be inside my head as well as another part of my body. Adam turned on his side and brushed my hair away from my forehead, 'You were a severe young woman when first I met you.'

'I was, wasn't I? But how could anyone stay serious living with you, Adam?'

'Maybe I'll become more serious, you know, more learned and all that. Would you like that?'

'More serious? Why would you want to? You're perfect just as you are.'

'That's true, of course, I am always telling you that... but I wish I could keep up with you intellectually. You know, literature and the poetry stuff you're really interested in.'

'Don't be ridiculous. I don't want to talk about photography. Anyway, I think you're fishing for compliments. Typical strategy, you criticise yourself waiting for me to praise you. I'm not going to fall into that trap.'

'Didn't think you would, Princess. I've been singing your praises though, so it would only be fair if you threw me one or two morsels of flattery.'

'What do you mean... oh no, you've been talking about me to the reporters, haven't you?'

'Maybe, purrtettrrre, as Bernie would say.'

'Tell me what you said, tell me every word.'

'Oh, I can't really remember... '

I swung my leg over Adam and sat on him and then began to tickle him. He had a terrible weakness for being tickled in his ribs.

'No, no, stop, stop. I give in. I'll tell you everything, stop.'

I relented and glared down at him, 'Go on then, tell me the worst.'

'Oh, my ribs. Do you know how much punishment my ribs suffer living with you? No, don't start again, I'll tell you. They wanted to know about the attack, of course. I told them that my wife might look like a fragile version of Greta Garbo, but she is more than a match for two low-life muggers on a scooter. That you sported a black belt in Taekwondo... oh yes, and that you were with a friend who was pregnant and you protected her. They loved that snippet.'

'I sank back on the bed, releasing Adam. 'You didn't. Oh god, now it will be in all the papers, I suppose.'

'Absolutely, I saw the guy from the Mail, I've known him a while, and the Times, he's a nice guy. There were quite a few I knew. Some top class paps there. They were all teasing me, of course, asking if you looked after me, too. There was a guy there from Le Figaro, I remember he was involved with that dreadful affair when Princess Diana was killed.'

I shuddered, 'I can't help thinking that Bernard is right, the paparazzi are like a flock of vultures.'

'Oh, is that what he said?' Adam shook his head, 'Nah, they're just doing their job, you know. Anyway, Melanie will be pleased with me even if Bernard doesn't approve.'

'Melanie, oh yes, goodness, we must tell her.'

'Tell her? Don't you realise she set it all up? She's building up your image in the Greta Garbo style... you know, remote and unobtainable. Now she'll be able to work on deadly dangerous, too.'

I couldn't hold back a long sigh, 'For goodness sake, I'm just a wine writer. It's the TV appearances that have changed everything and then marrying a famous war photographer... now we are both caught in the headlights like rabbits.'

'Rather melodramatic, Princess, but then I guess that's Princessy thing. Limelight, not headlights and you manage very well at keeping a low profile. Melanie is clever, she manipulates your natural reluctance to flirt with publicity into an act of secrecy and aloofness.'

'Aloofness, gosh, that's quite a word, Adam. But I think you and Melanie are rather harsh on me. Until quite recently, I've lived in seclusion. I know you like the whole idea of my being a Greta Garbo lookalike but you know it's ridiculous. I just enjoy my privacy.'

'Exactly, like Garbo... her famous quote "I want to be alone." In fact, I read once that's a misquote and what she actually said was 'I want to be left alone.' There's all the difference, isn't there?'

'Definitely, but you know it's quite alarming how much you know about Garbo.'

'I've loved her since I was a kid. My dream woman, I had a great black and white photo of her in my school locker. Then, later, she was my photographer's dream... classic looks, perfect skin and such depth to her eyes. Can you imagine how it was for me to meet you, standing like an ice princess in that posh hotel in snowy Courchevel?.' Adam sat up and ran his finger over one of my eyebrows. 'And beautiful, beautiful eyebrows.'

I thought for a brief moment of our first meeting, and the scene played in my head like a trailer to a film. Every detail of the marble foyer in the hotel, the sparkling chandeliers, the bemused porter standing aside as Adam had strode into my life in his leather boots and Parka, snowflakes caught in his long blonde eyelashes. How he had looked at me, his cornflower blue eyes laughing at my surprise. The very moment he had started to thaw my frozen heart. I blinked rapidly to dismiss the image and said quickly,

'Well, I'm not sure I like to be a lookalike. I just want to be me.' I jumped off the bed, suddenly full of energy. 'I've just remembered, I bought you a little present in Recanati. Bernard retrieved it from the Leopardi Palazzo and I put it in the armoire.'

Adam bounced off the bed, 'Present for me? How could you forget?'

I decided not to reply that there had been other things on my mind but just opened the bag and took out the small neatly gift-wrapped parcel from the leather shop.

'It's only a little present. Here you are, my love.'

Adam ran to me and took it eagerly, immediately applied his teeth to the string knot. I briefly admired his muscular body as he stood in front of me, completely at ease in his nakedness. It was something that I loved about him, his natural lack of inhibition, that and his unawareness of his male beauty. Now he ripped open the wrapping and found the small, beautifully made leather box.

'So beautiful, look at the craftmanship, the smoothness of the leather and the stitching. Thank you, my love, it's lovely.' He kissed me gently on the mouth and then said, 'Luckily I have a little present for you, too.'

'Really, how did you manage that?'

'Johnny and I didn't waste our time in the café. We had our own little shopping spree. There was a jeweller in the piazza and I found you something. It's in my Parka pocket. Hold on.'

Now he ran across the room to where his Parka was hanging on a hook on the back of the door, giving me another opportunity to admire his athleticism. Then he dug into his pocket and found a very small package and came back to me and held it out.

'I took it, trying not to smile at the crumpled ribbon and creased wrapping paper. I pulled at the gold ribbon and the bow untied easily. Now, I felt a rush of excitement as Adam was very good at choosing presents. I looked up at him and saw he was looking nervous, wondering if I would like whatever was hiding inside. Finally I let the paper drop to the floor and held the small dark green velvet box in my hand. Then, I clicked it open and gave a small gasp of delight at the tiny ear-rings that nested inside. Yes, Adam was very, very good at choosing presents. I gave Adam a quick kiss and then went to the mirror.

'They're so beautiful, Adam. Such tiny bunches of grapes… are they antique?'

Now, Adam looking very pleased with himself, stood behind me, looking into the mirror as I carefully fitted the ear-rings into my ears, he said, 'Well, the jeweller said they were art-deco. The grapes are tiny rubies, emeralds and… something else, oh, I know, amethyst. Pretty, aren't they?'

'Lovely, absolutely lovely. So delicate. Thank you, my love.'

'When you're not wearing them you can keep them in my box, if you want.?'

'Thank you, I'd like to do that. Both together will be a good memento of our time here.' I turned away from admiring myself in the mirror and kissed Adam again. I suddenly realised that Adam really had nothing of his own to put in the box. Why hadn't I thought of that? Apart from photographic equipment, Adam owned very little indeed. I thought about it for a moment and found myself drifting into an internal debate on the value of possessions. Then, I became aware that Adam was still standing close to me and looking at my new ear-rings. He reached out his hands and gently pushed my hair back behind my ears as he said quietly,

'Trouble is, Princess, there is nothing on earth beautiful enough for you.'

I shook my head, letting my hair fly out again. 'Do stop being so irresistible, Adam. I'm really going to look through my notes now.'

Adam took a step backward and saluted me, again not thinking about his complete nudity, 'Yes, ma-am. Absolutely, ma-am. How could I forget, you were going to let me help you collate. Why does that word sound so... so...'

'It doesn't sound so anything. Now, you go and play with your tablet.'

'Even that sounds sort of...'

'No, it really doesn't.'

Now, it was Adam's turn to heave a huge sigh.

That evening we found Rowena and Johnny with Luigi in the anteroom to the dining room. A fire had been lit, the heavy brocade curtains drawn closed and the room had the warmth of elegant opulence. Johnny and Luigi both stood as we walked in and I was struck by the likeness of the two young men, both tall, handsome and elegant in a wealthy Italian way. It was no wonder that Adam had thought to introduce them to each other. They could easily have been brothers. Rowena, sitting in a small velvet armchair at the fireside looked up and smiled,

'Isn't it lovely to have a log fire. I love the approach of Autumn.'

I smiled back and took the chair on the other side of the fireplace, thinking there was nothing that could ruffle Rowena's quiet happiness.

'Yes, lovely,' I answered, 'But I think there is a storm on its way. The clouds are very dark over the sea.'

'Well, it won't affect us here, will it?' Rowena continued still smiling.

I decided to change the subject as there was only so much sweet self-satisfaction I felt I could stand. 'How was your day at Recanati?'

'Oh, very good.'

Rowena's short response annoyed me for no sensible reason. I nodded and tried a saccharine smile and then turned to Johnny who was talking with Adam and Luigi.

'You should have been there, Eve. I don't suppose the lecture would have been at your level, but it was interesting.'

'Oh, don't think that. There is always something new to learn. In fact, I did attend a week of lectures at the Leopardi museum when I was in my first year at Cambridge. But it all seems like the distant past now.'

Luigi, who was now lounging on an eighteenth-century sofa, every centimetre a young aristocrat, said,

'I never knew they gave lectures at all, even though I live so near. Today was amazing.'

I looked at him with interest, waiting for him to add his favourite word, cool. Even though he was lolling back against the silk fringed cushions, a glass of water in his hand, there was a certain change in his face. Had he already decided to change his ways? My internal question was immediately answered as he said,

'Rowena and Johnny have been such great company. It's made me realise how bored I am living at my parent's farm. The truth is, I'm not the slightest bit keen on wine.' He raised his glass to his lips and smiled, flashing his perfect teeth for a second as he added, 'I hate to say it to you, Eve, but I prefer a good rye whisky.'

I laughed, his charm was somewhat irresistible, 'Everyone has different tastes, Luigi, that's something I always try to remember. Your father does make extraordinarily good wine, though.'

'I guess so, yeah, I know it really. More due to my grandfather than my Pa. He just picked up the reins when my Nonno died. If the will hadn't specified that the vineyard should continue to be worked in the traditional way, I bet my father would have wrecked it by now. He'd like a laboratory of chemicals to play around with.'

I looked at Luigi with interest and wanted to ask more as it did seem to have a ring of truth. From the little time I had spent with Signor Marioni it was obvious he was not a lover of tradition. However, the conversation turned back to their day in Recanati as Rowena said,

'We saw Bernard in the square outside the museum, but we didn't speak. He was in the midst of a group of uniformed police. Carabinieri I suppose.'

Adam spoke as he sat down on the window seat, 'That's Bernie, always on the prowl. He has never properly retired from the police force. He's been meeting his mates in Ancona, I know he's still worried about something sinister around here.' He moved aside the heavy curtain and looked out into the darkness. 'I think you're right, Eve, there's a storm brewing.' As he spoke, there was a distant rumble of thunder, and the lights in the room flickered.

'A good storm will clear the air.' Rowena said cheerily. I closed my eyes briefly, wondering if there was anything that could change her rosy view. Rosy Rowena. I thought to myself, how would it feel to be so resolutely content?

The lights flickered again, and a young girl came in to light the candles in the wall sconces. I briefly wondered how Rowena would handle an electric blackout, but before I could continue my rather unkind thought, the door opened, and Bernard entered, smiling broadly.

'*Bonsoir, tout le monde. Vous êtes bien installés, une soirée douillettes au coin du feu.*'

We all looked up at him, and there was a general feeling of relief and delight that he was back with us and happy to be so. As he said with one of his rare broad smiles, he was very pleased to find us all sitting so cosily together in the firelight.

The evening continued well, everyone in good humour and the food as excellent as ever. Luigi emerged from his cool and became an interesting and amusing guest... until near the end of the meal. When desserts were served, he disappeared off, and I noticed Adam and Johnny exchange glances. Adam stood up, but Johnny said,

'It's OK, Adam, I've got this. Let me go.'

Johnny gave Rowena a quick kiss and then left the table. We sat in silence for a minute, and I felt my spirits sink. Bernard was the first to speak.

'Luigi is a good young man, but he needs the help. *Non*?'

'Indeed he does.' Adam said, his face serious and sad, 'I think Johnny is the man to be there for him. What do you think, Rowena?'

'Absolutely! I know Johnny will sort him out. He knows what to do. We'll get Luigi to England and into detox. He'll be fine.'

I looked at Rowena with curiosity. Her sweet Madonna face was smiling, and her hands were folded together on her baby bump, utterly relaxed. Did nothing ruffle her?

Before I could say anything, Luigi and Johnny returned to the table. Now I looked at Luigi with interest as he sat down. Yes, the pupils of his dark eyes were dilated, and he seemed to buzz with excitement. I looked at Adam, thinking that he should have gone with Luigi as obviously Johnny had not been successful in stopping Luigi from taking cocaine. Adam was chatting with Rowena and not looking at me. Then, my heart missing a beat, I looked closely at Johnny. Had he joined Luigi to share not stop? But Johnny seemed calm and quiet, patiently listening to Luigi as he excitedly rattled on about Leopardi's poem, *Zibaldone*.

    I felt suddenly alone and out of my depth. What was I doing here in such company? I yearned to be back in Provence in my own peaceful farmhouse, with my books and... then, I abruptly stopped my train of thought. What was I thinking? Why did I not long to be back in London, with Adam, my husband, in our new life together? I inhaled a deep breath and tried to relax my shoulders. Was breathing in the same as a sigh? I closed my eyes, as my head swam. Too many foolish notions in my head. Finally, a practical thought came to me. Had I enough material to finish my work here in Le Marche? Could I cut and run, flee from the troubles surrounding me? I flicked my eyes open as I felt Adam's hand rest on my shoulder.

    'Cheer up, Princess. We'll be back in your comfort zone soon. Day after tomorrow I'll be burning toast for you again. Me, I can't wait!'

    As usual, he had guessed my thoughts, and his words released some tight knot within me. I turned to him and smiled,

    'I can't wait either.' I lowered my head toward him and whispered, 'I love you, Adam.'

He responded with a quick kiss on the tip of my nose and said,

'I love you more, you know that. Now, on a more serious matter... are you going to finish your Tiramisu?'

I pushed my plate toward him, 'Is there no end to your appetite, Adam. You've already eaten Rowena's *panna cotta*.'

'I have an insatiable appetite for all the good things in life, Princess, you should know that.'

I felt the colour rush to my cheeks and to cover my confusion, I turned to Bernard.

'Did you speak to Elaine today, Bernard?'
'Mais oui, I speak every day, she send her love to you and Adam.'
'Thank you, I know she must miss you so much. I think my work is nearly finished here.'

Adam, turned to me, a spoonful of Tiramisu held halfway to his mouth, 'You think? What does that mean? You have all the notes you need, surely and I have more than enough photos. What do you mean, you think? Tell me, Princess?'

'Well,' I folded and refolded my napkin as I hesitated to reply and then said awkwardly, 'Well, I'm just a little concerned. The Marioni Verdicchio is excellent, no doubt about that but...'
I hesitated for a moment, and Luigi stood up, his hands resting on the table as he said, 'But... my father is a monster? That's what's worrying you, isn't it?'

Now there was an awkward silence, and then Johnny tugged at Luigi's arm and persuaded him to sit down again.

'Calm down, Luigi, I'm sure that's not what Eve is worried about.'

Luigi looked straight across the table at me, and there was a depth of sadness in his dark eyes that made me want to cry. I knew something about missing father love. In fact, in my life, I had missed mother love, too. Everyone around the table was now looking at me, waiting for my reply. I spoke slowly,

'Actually, I think Luigi has exactly recognised my source of worry. I'm not sure I had even recognised it myself until he spoke.'

Luigi was still looking at me and me alone as I continued carefully, 'You see, in my travels for the book I'm writing with Adam, we've met all sorts of people. It's not my job to write about them, I write about wine but...' I hesitated, 'but if I am to sign my name on the label of the next vintage... well, obviously I need to know that the quality of the wine will continue.'

Luigi now nodded enthusiastically, his long dark hair shining in the candlelight, 'Exactly, Eve, exactly. That's integrity, right?'

'Right,' I nodded back at him, thinking integrity was a vast improvement on cool. But his next excited words surprised me,

'You don't need to worry, Eve. The wines at Casa Verde will always stick to tradition. My mother sees to that.' Luigi now slumped back in his chair as though he had exhausted all his wild energy.

Adam sat forward to gain Luigi's attention. 'Your mother? Does your mother have a hand in the business, Luigi?'

'Sure, in her own quiet way she runs the place. She grew up on a wine farm in the Napa Valley, and she knows the business. My wretched father just picks up the medals and sails off again into the blue. Mamma and I both know he has a girlfriend in Porto Recanati and they go off together on his huge flashy yacht. I tell you, he's a monster, and my Mamma is a saint.'

Now, Luigi reached for the decanter of cognac that was in the centre of the table. It was Rowena's hand that stretched out quickly and pushed it out of his reach. Then, she spoke very quietly,

'Enough, Luigi, basta. We are all your friends here, and we are going to help you. Johnny, go and arrange a room for Luigi here for tonight. Tomorrow, Luigi, we will go with you to Casa Verde and collect your things. I'll speak with your mother and tell her you are coming to England with us. Everything will be arranged. Do you understand?'

Luigi nodded, quietly and to my dismay, I saw that tears were rolling down his tanned cheeks. Johnny left the table as commanded and then Bernard stood up,

'I wish you all the good night. I think we speak again at the breakfast, yes? Is late now to make the plans for your work, Mademoiselle Eve. *Demain il fera jour, n'est ce pas?*'

I stood up feeling incredibly tired, 'Yes, tomorrow is another day, Bernard. *A demain et bonne nuit.*'

It was already tomorrow when we said goodnight to the others at just after midnight. The usual jokes were made about pumpkins and fairy godmothers as we made our way to our rooms. I noticed the Johnny had his arm over Luigi's shoulders as they walked away from us in the long first-floor corridor. Adam must have noticed, too, as he said quietly,

'Looks like Rowena and Johnny are determined to take care of young Luigi.'

'All due to you getting them together in the first place, Adam. You do work in mysterious ways. I am proud of you.'

Adam spun on one heel to face me as we continued to stroll along the corridor, 'Really? Proud of me? Holy Moly, I think I'm blushing.' He had turned and was walking backwards toward the window at the end of the corridor. I took a moment to admire the angular outline of his body as he jogged backwards, arms outstretched to me.

'I don't think you're blushing, Adam, but you do look very pleased with yourself.'

We reached our bedroom door, and Adam stopped, but I put my hand on his shoulder, turning him a little as I said, 'Have you looked out of the window at the end there?'

Adam turned right around and said, 'Yes, I took some photos from there the other morning. Wonderful view.'

'It is, isn't it. The architect of the Villa certainly knew how to make the most of an aspect. I looked out the other day and saw you coming back from talking with the journalists. Shall we look now?'

We carried on, hand in hand to the end of the corridor and looked out. There was a full moon half obscured by scudding clouds. The wind, blowing in from the sea, was causing the orange trees to sway and bend In the distance the treetops of the forest were lashing back and forth. I think we both noticed at the same time the flash of bright light that came from the low flat-roofed building that nestled in a small opening in the trees.

'Did you see that?' Adam grabbed my hand and added, That wasn't lightning, was it?'

'No, I saw exactly the same the other night. Definitely not lightning, but a short flash on yellow electric light then nothing.'

We stood side by side in silence, waiting to see the light flash again, but nothing happened. We waited for another few minutes and then Adam broke the silence,

'I think that must be the building where I met that dog. I wonder what's going on down there?'

I held my breath, hesitating before I replied, not wanting to show too much interest as I knew Adam would want to go out into the night and investigate. His incurable curiosity had led us into so many difficult situations. But there was a problem, and the real reason for my hesitation was my own spirit of inquisitiveness.

'Hmm, yes...' I murmured, 'Curiouser and curiouser.'

Adam squeezed my hand and said, 'OK, Alice-Eve, I know what it means when you forget your English grammar. I can't see a white rabbit, but I think I'm just going to take a walk.'

'Me, too.' I added quickly, 'Don't try your usual trick of leaving me behind. I'm coming too.'

'Definitely not, Princess. Bernard would have my guts for garters if he knew I let you take a midnight walk.'

'Let me? Can you hear yourself? No-one ever has or ever will stop me from doing what I want.'

'OK, OK, hair on Princess! I can't be bothered to go out there anyway, let's go to bed.'

I looked at Adam suspiciously as he rarely capitulated so easily.

'Hmm, I agree, time for bed, then.'

We both turned away from the window and strolled back to our room. Adam slipped his arm around my waist and ducked to kiss my neck as he opened the door. The touch of his lips on my skin made me immediately forget any thought of light flashing from the forest or, indeed, anything apart from desire. He was softly murmuring my name over and over as we fell together onto the bed and began to pull off our clothes. My dress had a long zip down the back, and as Adam slowly pulled it down, he kissed the length of my spine until I was shuddering and longing for him to be inside me. We made fast, almost violent love and then fell apart, panting and satisfied.

I took Adam's hand in mine and kissed it, still unable to speak but wanting to tell him how much I loved him. He sat up, kissed my hand and then said,

'I'll get you a glass of water, my love, just a minute.'

I lay still, my eyes half closed but watching him move across the room. Yet another opportunity to admire his physical elegance. Something animal, athletic and powerful yet light as a dancer. He returned with a bottle of water from the small fridge and poured me a glass. I sipped it gratefully and then sank back onto the pillows, exhausted. Adam lay beside me, and soon I fell into a dreamless sleep.

I awoke, with no idea how long I had slept but knowing that Adam was no longer beside me in our bed. I sat up quickly, just in time to hear the bedroom door close very quietly. Instantly I knew that Adam had gone to explore the light in the forest. I exhaled sharply, a sigh of sheer exasperation, and then I was up, pulling on a t-shirt and jeans, pushing my feet into my boots and finally, grabbing my anorak, I ran to the door to follow Adam.

29

The corridor was half-lit by dimmed wall lights, and I ran past the lift to the staircase at the far end. I stopped for a moment at the top, holding the bannister and peering down into the hall below. There was no sound, so I slipped noiselessly down the first flight, my footsteps muffled by the thick carpet. On the large half-landing, I stopped again as I hear the click of a door lock. Again, I leant over the bannister to peer into the half darkness, but nothing moved. I ran down the last flight and through the hall to the front door. There was a small room on the right where the footman always attended the door. I moved cautiously forward to look through the small panes of the window and saw the young man that so often served us was fast asleep, his head resting on the desk in front of him. I smiled to myself, thinking how Bernard would be appalled at the Villa's security. Then, I tried the handle of the front door, and it opened easily. I guessed that Adam had left it unlocked, ready for his return. I slipped through and closed it carefully behind me. The air was cold, and I pulled on my anorak and zipped it up to my chin, pulling the hood over my head. The wind was still blowing strongly, and the moon shone as bright as day. I made out the familiar figure of Adam, his Parka flapping around him like a wayward tent. He was marching down the centre of the drive, and I ran after him, dodging between the orange trees for cover. My heart was beating with excitement and the enjoyable thought of tricking Adam. As he reached the high gates, he turned, and I was caught between orange trees.

'You don't honestly think I don't know you're following me, do you, Princess?'

I caught up with him and grasped the sleeve of his Parka, giving it a good shake. 'And you don't honestly think you can slip away and leave me out of the fun, do you?'

Adam rested his hands on my shoulders and looked down at me, the moonlight glinting in his blue eyes, 'Is there any point at all in telling you... sorry, asking you, to go back to the Villa?'

I shook my head, my hood slipping down and allowing my hair to fly wildly in the wind. Adam leant down and quickly kissed me on the end of my nose and pulled my hood up again and fastened the string below my chin. I took this as a sign of acceptance, and as he strode on, I hurried to run after him again. He had the advantage of very long legs, but I had spent many hours running and jogging around Hyde Park, and I could have overtaken him if I wanted. Once outside the gates, Adam turned immediately to the left, following a small sandy downhill path. There was more shelter from the wind as we reached the edge of the forest, but the first drops of rain began to fall. Adam stopped abruptly, and I was so close behind that I bumped into him. He put his arms around me and muttered,

'Come on, Eve, give up and go back. It's going to pour down.'

As though the weather was on his side, there was a small gust of wind carrying a splatter of icy raindrops straight into my face. It did seem entirely crazy to be out in the dark, and for one moment I thought about returning to the comfort of the Villa and our large bed.

'Only if you come with me, Adam.' I smiled in what I hoped was a sweet, beguiling way.

'No good trying that act, Princess. I'm as curious as the proverbial cat.'

'Well, if you're determined to get proverbially killed, then I'd better be there to save you.'

Adam sighed, and I added, 'You have a whole range of sighs, did you know that, Adam?'

My words provoked another sigh, and then Adam turned smartly on his heel and carried on down the path.

We must have walked in silence for nearly five minutes, keeping up a good pace without running until I saw a gateway ahead. There was a chain stretched across the opening… and then I remembered the dog.

Adam turned to me and said, 'I'll go ahead and talk to Butterscotch, OK?'

'Butterscotch?' I repeated feebly, but I stood stock still as there was low growl and a dog that could have played the part of the Hound of the Baskervilles strolled casually onto centre stage and then stood still, paws planted solidly in the sandy gravel and eyes catching the moonlight. I had a strong inclination to turn and run but something half-remembered from a safari trip with my father came to me, and I sank to the ground. Adam moved forward slowly, bent low and softly calling the name Butterscotch To my utter relief the dog began to wag his tail and wriggle toward Adam, as though he was a cute puppy. I saw Adam hold out his hand and the dog very politely took his snack. Butterscotch, I wondered?

Adam beckoned to me, and I rose slowly from my uncomfortable position on the ground and scuttled slowly forward, keeping low. As I approached the dog looked up, and Adam stroked his big head and whispered something in his black floppy ear. I continued moving slowly forward until I reached Adam and muttered,

'Please don't tell me you are actually a dog whisperer.'

Adam shrugged and just said, 'Eve, meet my friend Butterscotch. Butterscotch this is the annoying Princess that I was telling you about. She follows me everywhere.'

The dog turned his head to study me closely, his dark brown eyes were surprisingly friendly beneath a rather sweet triangular frown. I thought to pat him but decided to err on the side of caution, and said, 'Pleased to meet you, Butterscotch, although I am guessing that is not actually your name.'

Adam stood up, and I cautiously rose to my full height to stand beside him and the dog, large paws still planted fair and square in the soil, stood between us. We all looked across the yard to a collection of dark buildings. Nothing moved, but there was the low throb of a generator and an old Suzuki Jeep parked at an angle in front of the nearest shed.

Suddenly, it felt foolish to be there at all, and I thought once more of the warm, comfortable bed awaiting us back at the Villa. Then, Adam took my hand and moved forward toward the Jeep. Butterscotch and I obediently kept with him until he stopped again and raised one finger to his lips. The moonlight was still as bright, and I saw Adam's eyebrows raised as he listened. I remained very still, and then over the continual hum of the generator, I made out the sound of muffled music, heavy metal, maybe or electronic rock? The bass sound reverberated and came to us on a gust of wind. I clutched Adam's sleeve and whispered,

'There's someone inside, I can hear music. Let's go back to the Villa!' I tugged frantically at a fold of Adam's Parka, but he shook his head.

'I told you not to come, Princess. Too late now to go back on your own.'

I gave another jag at his Parka, angry now and not sure whether it was his I-told-you-so voice or the fact that he thought I couldn't find my own way back to the Villa. I moved quickly away from the shelter of the Jeep and ran to the nearest building. Adam and Butterscotch followed me, and we all moved along until we reached a window. A window that might as well have been a wall as it was tightly closed and shuttered but now the music was slightly louder. Adam now pulled at my sleeve, and I turned to look at him. He was gesturing to the next window along, and I saw there was a very narrow strip of light along the bottom. We moved slowly toward it, Butterscotch commendably entering our game of silence by scuttling along on his huge paws, with his tongue lolling out of his open mouth as though to breathe more silently.

As soon as we reached the next window, Adam squatted down to peer into the narrow strip of light. I caught up with him and did the same and then drew in my breath sharply and turned to Adam. He was looking at me with a face that expressed the same shock that I was feeling. We had both looked in on the evils of a cocaine factory. I gasped and clutched again at Adam' sleeve, peering through the thin gap at the scene was laid out in front of us. It was a long room, brightly lit by fluorescent tubes suspended over a line of stainless steel tables. There were four young women, clad only in their underwear, green shower caps and white masks, shovelling small piles of white powder into green polythene bags. A man, wearing a white all-in-one overall and a weird animal mask was strutting around between the women, moving in time to the loud beat of the electronic music and clutching a rifle. He stopped once to check the time on his wristwatch, and I saw a flash of gold. Then he resumed his pacing, pushing one of the girls in the back with the end of his rifle. The scene was equal to any vision of hell, the horrific look of a Hieronymus Bosch painting or a vision of Dante's hell. I sank back on my heels, suddenly unable to look any longer.

Adam took my hand and tugged me to move away. Still crouching low and with Butterscotch following closely at our heels, we moved silently away from the window. I wanted to run away, run and run back to the safety and luxury of the Villa, but Adam still held my hand and pulled me toward the next building. We stayed silent, whether because we were too shocked to speak or if it was the fear of being heard... I wasn't sure. I reluctantly followed Adam until we were up close to the wall of the next building. Now there were no windows, just a high corrugated door, large enough for lorries. I looked at Adam, wondering why he wanted to find out more. Surely, all we needed to do was to get away safely and call the police? Rain was falling faster now, plastering the hair that had escaped from my hood onto my forehead.

I was about to tell Adam that we had to go, that we must leave, when the large door moved upwards, the sound of its rust mechanism filling the air and the flash of light from within suddenly falling on us. I gave a small scream and then saw Adam slump to the ground as a dark figure, holding a gun, stood over him. Then, someone grabbed me from behind. I reacted instinctively and kicked backwards but then a hand clutched my mouth, and I smelt the sickly sweet smell of chloroform. I struggled for a moment, trying to twist my head as my face was sprayed with an icy liquid. I managed to bite the hand through the cloth over my mouth, but then, as my knees gave way and I felt myself falling into a dark void.

30

I heard my own voice crying out, trying to scream but my throat was too dry. Had I made any noise at all or was it in my dream? My head was throbbing with pain or was it my heart beating so loud that it sounded in my ears. Gradually, very slowly I managed to raise my eyelids. Everything was black, inky dark and terrifying. Was I dead? I closed my eyes again, my eyelashes feeling heavy as though weighted. My brain began to race with frightening speed. I had been outside in the yard at the cocaine farm, and someone had attacked me, yes, that was it, someone had grabbed me from behind and held a cloth over my mouth. My brain struggled with the information and then cleared... chloroform. Yes, I had been drugged with chloroform... maybe ether? I ran my tongue around my dry mouth and remembered the sweet sickly smell. I was not dead. I had been next to Adam... suddenly I flicked my eyes open as I remembered. Adam had fallen to the ground beside me... there had been a man with a gun pointing down at him... Adam was dead. Now I cried out, and this time I heard myself make a strange animal sound that I had never made before. I struggled to move but found my hands tightly fastened behind me.

Now, with my eyes stretched wide open in absolute dread, I saw the darkness was not quite complete. There was a dim red glow high above me. I stared at it and finally focused on the word Exit, black letters on a red square of light. Some sort of security light? As my eyes gradually, very gradually, became accustomed to the dimness I began to look around. Then, I froze into horrified stillness. Adam was lying on the floor beside me, perfectly still, so still and... lifeless. As I struggled again to move, I heard panting, and my blood froze in my veins. There was someone else very near me. I forced myself to look again at Adam's body as it lay beside me. He was lying face down, and his Parka hood covered his head, just one long blonde curl escaped, but he made no movement. Then I heard a shuffling sound, and I drew my knees in up to my chin, trying to shrink back against whatever was holding my hands. I felt the hard shape of a radiator press into my back. So I was tied to a radiator. My brain processed the information, but it was of no interest to me. With Adam dead, I had no wish to survive. I closed my eyes again and tried not to listen to the words of Juliet that played in my head,

"O, here will I set up my everlasting rest, and shake the yoke of inauspicious stars from this world-wearied flesh."

I gave a shuddering sigh and thought then of poor Ophelia. I wanted to die not to go mad from utter misery.

The shuffling sound broke through my crazy thoughts and now, the panting had turned to some kind of snuffling, licking sound.

'Butterscotch!' I said the word aloud, and my eyes flew open as I strained to see in the murky darkness. Yes, there was the large dog beside Adam's body, carefully licking Adam's left hand that was outstretched as though reaching out to me. Now, I could see Adam's long fingers and on one, the gleam of the wedding ring I had given him.

Butterscotch stopped his licking and turned to look at me. The red light caught in his eyes under the tan patches of his eyebrows. He looked at me for a long moment, his face sad and gentle, then he returned to his carefully licking of Adam's hand. I stared in horrid fascination and then just as I was about to look away I saw Adam's thumb make a flickering movement. I screamed,

'Adam, Adam!' My voice was my own, and it rang out loud and clear, loud enough to make Adam roll onto his side and say in a low voice.

'Princess? Are you all right?'

Now, tears were streaming down my cheeks as I replied,

'Yes, I'm all right, I think.'

Adam stirred again and then slowly sat up, looked at me and patted Butterscotch's large head,

'You OK, Butterscotch?'

The dog wagged his thick stubby tail in answer and sat back on his haunches almost smiling. Adam rubbed his head and then said again,

'You OK, Princess?' then added, 'Oh my God, if we get out of here alive then Bernie's going to kill me anyway.'

I gave a heavy sigh, a sigh that surely covered the whole catalogue of sighs. I blinked rapidly, trying to flick away the tears filling my eyes.

'No, actually, I most definitely am not OK, My head is throbbing, I'm sitting on the floor of some filthy shed in the dark with my hands tied behind me...' my voice broke as I added, 'and I thought you were dead.'

'Oh sweet Princess, that's horrible, but you do sound more yourself now, ackchewally.' He drew himself up onto his knees and shuffled over to me and kissed my nose. 'You're in a fine state, aren't you. Hold on, let me see your poor little hands.'

'Can't see anything in here.' I replied in a stupid, sulky voice. My relief in finding that Adam was alive had quickly turned to irrational anger, 'This is all your fault, Adam. We should have run back to the Villa and called the police and...' I stopped speaking abruptly as I found my hands had been freed and Adam was gently massaging my wrists.

Then I began to sob as I circled his neck and pulled him close to me. 'I thought you were dead, there was a man with a gun and...'

'Take more than a sucker-punch and a taser gun to kill me off, Princess. But...' Adam stood up now and held out his hand to pull me to my feet, 'But I don't think you are the only person to think me dead. I guess I would have been tied up too if they thought I was alive. Which means, Princess, they have something in mind for you. Ransom, maybe?'

Adam rubbed his eyes and put his arms on my shoulders,

'Whatever, we've seen too much to be left alive. Besides, I'm clean out of butterscotch sweeties. We have to get out of here and quickly... you, too,

Butterscotch. You're in big trouble as a failed guard dog.' Adam leant down and fondled the dog's ears and then added, 'Chop, chop, Princess, see that word Exit up there in red light? It's trying to tell us something. Let's go!'

Of course, it wasn't as easy as all that. The door proved to be solidly locked, but after five minutes which seemed like five hours, Adam managed to pick the lock and then very cautiously open the door. Immediately, cold rain blew into our faces as we peered into the new outside darkness. I gulped in the fresh air and pulled up the hood of my anorak. I tried to move past Adam, but he held my arm,

'Wait, wait, there may be some security system.. bound to be.'

So I waited, dreading to hear an alarm or find ourselves caught in a security light.

'There was nothing before when we came into the yard.' I whispered, 'I think they rely on Butterscotch.'

'I guess so, OK, let's make a run for it. We'll take the Jeep.'

I grabbed Adam's arm, 'The Jeep? There won't be any keys in it, surely. No, let's run back to the Villa.'

But Adam was already running across the yard, splashing through the puddles and with Butterscotch lumbering along at his heels. I had no choice than to follow. I caught up as Adam opened the driver's door of the old Jeep. I wrenched open the passenger door, and Butterscotch dived in before me. I sat on the front seat, with my arm around the bulky body of the dog for comfort. Adam was messing around under the steering wheel, and I said angrily,

'I told you they wouldn't leave the keys in the ignition, Adam, it would better to...'

My words were drowned out by the sound of the engine firing into life. Adam threw the gear stick into reverse, and we rocketed across the yard and then swung around and drove straight out of the gates. I looked back anxiously, imagining a film scene with bullets flying after us, shattering the windows but there was nothing at all. Then the yard and the cluster of buildings was lit by a flash of lightning followed immediately by an ear-splitting clap of thunder. I shuddered and held Butterscotch closer to me as the Jeep jagged and bumped out of the yard. A squall of rain hit the windscreen as Adam turned on the headlights and swung on to the sandy lane. He turned to me and smiled, a tired but still charmingly wonky smile as he said,

'Thank the Gods for electro-rock music! They won't have heard a thing.'

31

I didn't care what time it was, there was no way that I was getting up. I pulled the covers completely over my head and curled up into a tight ball, clutching the sheet tight in case Adam decided differently. He was talking at me, his voice now taking on a wheedling tone,

'... and anyway, Princess, you can't leave me to face Bernie alone. He'll have my guts for garters, and I'll end up in a fountain again. You can tell him that I told you not to follow me, you know, he's never that angry with you.'

I made no reply but burrowed my head further into the soft pillow. Adam continued relentlessly,

'And the police will probably come back. You'll have to get up then.' He paused, 'I expect you're quite hungry, too?'

I wriggled in annoyance as he was right, I was, in fact, starving.

After we had escaped and returned to the safety of the Villa, Adam had rung Bernard, and he had rushed off, calling the police as he went. Less than an hour later we had heard the police sirens down in the forest as the police raided the farm. We had watched the commotion from the landing window, too tired to sleep and over-excited by the night's events. There had been one brief call back from Bernard to say that arrests had been made and that he would see us for breakfast.

Now, Adam was in a blue funk about being reprimanded by Bernard. Really, for a grown man, it was quite ridiculous. I turned over onto my back and stretched, pulling the sheet back so that I could squint with one eye at Adam as he paced around the room. and said,

'How come you can face tasers and Rottweilers and what was it... being sucker-punched and yet be scared or what Bernard will say to you?'

'Well, only one taser and one Rottweiler and he's such a sweetie, aren't you Buttie-Scottie?'

I sighed as I remembered that Butterscotch had spent the night on the carpet on Adam's side of the bed, and added,

'Not to mention hot-wiring and stealing a drug gangsters Jeep so...'

'Well, it seemed to be the only vehicle there so I thought if they had heard us escape they wouldn't be able to follow us.'

I sat up as I thought about it, 'Hmm, I suppose that was a good idea. Although I still think we should have left as soon as we looked in in that dreadful cocaine factory room.' I shuddered at the memory,

'Somehow the harsh white light and all the white powder made it so horrific... and the masks... oh my God, and those poor girls...' I faltered to a halt and Adam came and sat beside me on the bed and stroked my hair back from my forehead.

'It's all over, Princess and you need some food inside you, come on, chop chop. I'll find you something to wear.'

These last words made me laugh out loud, and I began to feel better.

'Very well, I'll come down to breakfast, but I shall definitely choose my own clothes.'

Adam was already standing by the tall armoire in the dressing room of our suite. He pulled out a red dress that I seldom wore but had packed in case there was an unexpected formal dinner.

'This looks great... why don't you wear this?'

'Because it is covered in sequins and only suitable for a very formal dinner. Really, Adam. I thought you knew about fashion.'

Adam held the dress up to himself and danced around the room singing in a falsetto Julie Andrew's voice, 'Princessy dresses and silky Rottweilers, Butterscotch sweeties and gold wedding rings, these are a few of my favourite things...'

I burst out laughing and gave in. When Adam was in this mood, usually because he was wired with nerves, there was nothing to do but to go with it.

Less than half an hour later, and to my surprise, no later than ten o'clock, we entered the breakfast room together. I had worn a red silk shirt to appease Adam, and apart from being ravenous, I now felt quite recovered.

Bernard, Johnny and Luigi stood up as we came up to the breakfast table and we all embraced. Rowena seated at the table, calm and serene as usual, held out her hand to me, saying,

'Eve, are you all right? You look fine, but you must be exhausted. Are you hungry? Here, let me pour you an orange juice and I can recommend the scrambled eggs.'

\She lifted the silver cover of a large platter of deep yellow eggs and carefully spooned a large portion onto a plate for me, adding, 'Just sit down and eat up. Bernard has told us most of the night's wild events, but you can tell us more when you've had some food. Now, how about you, Adam?'

I sat down gratefully and did exactly as she said, thinking to myself that Rowena would surely be an excellent mother. She served Adam an even more generous portion of eggs and added several slices of ham. I noticed he sat down quickly with a brief nod to Bernard. After I had eaten a few mouthfuls of the delicious creamy eggs, I looked up at Bernard who had remained standing,

'How did it go last night, Bernard, after you left us at the Villa?'

'Was the perfect bust, Mademoiselle Eve, perfect police work. Everyone arrested, taken by complete surprise. My friend is very, very pleased. Is very important find.'

I nodded and said, 'Adam was amazing, I'm sure he saved my life.'

At these words, Adam stopped eating and looked anxiously at Bernard as he said,

'Honestly, Bernie, I tried to stop Eve from following me but...'

Bernard went to stand behind Adam and patted him on the shoulder,

'But is impossible to stop her, I know, I know, *je comprends très bien*. Always she refuse to do as she is told. *Toujours impossible!*'

Adam looked at me across the table, his eyebrows raised in surprise and then gave a smile of pure relief before continuing to attack his ham and eggs.

I decided not to object to their shared disapproval of my behaviour, though why either of them should think that I needed to obey them was beyond me. Fortunately for them, I was still in a euphoric state of release from the fear and danger of the previous night.

Bernard sat down next to Luigi and cleared his throat. I realised there was something more that Bernard wanted to say, something important. I put my knife and fork together, pushed away my plate, sipped my orange juice and then said,

'What is it Bernard, what is worrying you?'

'Is very difficult what I have to say now.' Again, he gave a small cough. I looked at him anxiously as it was very rare for Bernard to be ill at ease. Then he said in a quiet voice, 'I am very sorry, Luigi, but I must tell you now. The boss man at the cocaine factory, the armed man in the animal mask was your father, Signor Marioni.'

'I thought Luigi took it well considering.' Adam and I had gone out for a walk in the gardens of the Villa. The sun had returned, and the world seemed washed clean by last night's violent storm.

'Yes, he did, but then there is no love lost between his father and himself, is there?' I gave a long sigh as I thought about it and the difficult time I often had loving my own father.

'That was a huge sigh, Princess. Probably needs t be added to the list. Sounded a bit wistful and a bit exhausted. Still, I know how you feel and probably how Luigi feels, too. My own Dad was arrested a couple of times for breaking and entering. I don't remember feeling anything much except that he had asked for it.'

I squeezed Adam's arm as we walked along the path between the rose beds, but remained silent. How could I say anything? My own anger at my father's disappearance after his meteoric fall from grace seemed to dwindle into insignificance. Now that it had been proved in the courts that he was innocent of all charges of fraud, my father was back almost to his former power. Well, not literally back to London. I stifled another sigh as I thought how he had settled so far away in Kerala, building a new life with his green tourist village. Then, I remembered that Adam had said he was still in London.

'Adam, did you say that my father was in London?'

'Yeah, last time I spoke to Lucinda he was there with her. I guess she's managed to get him involved with our project. She's a brilliant fund-raiser as well as a first-rate photographer. Of course, she knows all the right people.'

I subdued the usual twinge of jealousy that I felt whenever Adam praised Lucinda, and said,

'Yes, yes, I see that, and I expect Pa would be happy to invest in anything to set young people on the right path but still...' I hesitated, remembering how, when I had last seen my father, he had been anxious to return to India.

Adam nodded and said, 'You know he agreed to pose for a portrait session for a group of youngsters. I expect he got involved. Isn't that the sort of thing you say he always does?'

'Hmm, well, he does swoop in and take over things if he gets a chance. Will you mind if he has?'

'Mind? Good God, no. The project needs all the backing it can get. The brain of a brilliant businessman would be great input. Luc and I are basically photographers and no nothing about money matters. She's just a hoity-toity version of me.'

This made me laugh aloud as I could hardly imagine two more different people that my old school friend, the wealthy and spoilt Lucinda Sackville-Jones, a recovering alcoholic and my own sweet Adam. I decided to swerve the conversation and said,

'Hoity-toity? Hoit from the early English dialect meaning to play the fool. That's such a great rhyming reduplicated phrase?'

'If you say so, I'm sure it is. I just like the sound of it.'
'Exactly. Very pleasing, you know, like hoi-poloi... although that's a mistaken connection of course as 'poloi' comes from the Greek.'
'Of course it does, I'm sure I knew that.' Adam turned and kissed the tip of my nose. 'I'm so glad you're back on track, Princess Clever Clogs.'

I was still thinking about the meaning of hoity, so I was surprised when he continued, saying,

'Maybe when we've finished here and the next two assignments in Bardolino and Bordeaux, you know, maybe then you can return to your poetry. All that clever *terza rima* stuff?'

I gave his arm another affectionate squeeze and said,
'I think I might, you know. I do have some ideas floating around in my head sometimes. I have the inkling of an idea to move on to writing a Petrarchan sonnet. You know... ' I spoke more to myself now and added dreamily, 'a lyric love poem. I need to reread Horace's odes... yes, that would be so interesting.'

Adam was silent, and we reached the end of the rose walk and turned to take the gravel path that led uphill and back to the Villa. The ground was strewn with petals that had been blown by the strong gusts of wind in the night. The air was fresh, and I knew from experience that the heat of the summer had come to an end. It was the same in Provence where I had spent so much time. Now the days would be warm but no longer the fierce heat of summer. My

English blood enjoyed the release, and I felt a surge of energy and pure happiness. I turned to tell Adam and found he was already looking at me, holding out a small rosebud. He placed it in the buttonhole of my shirt and then said,

'Do you think you will be happy living with me, Eve?'

I stretched my eyes wide in surprise and said quickly, 'I was just thinking how very happy I am. I have never been happier than being with you. What made you say that?'

Adam turned away from me and scuffed the rose petals on the gravel with the toe of his boot. 'I dunno, you really are such a brilliant clever-clogs, and I'm a bit of a dolt, hoiting around with my camera.'

'Are you fishing for compliments again, Adam Wright? Considering you have received awards for your work?'

'Maybe I am.' Adam threw his arm across my shoulders and hugged me as we continued to walk uphill. 'And maybe you could give me another of your poetry lessons when we get back to our room?'
'That sounds like an excellent idea, my love.' I stretched up and kissed Adam's cheek and added, 'I can't wait. I can tell you all about the Petrarchan rhyme scheme.'

But as we reached the entrance to the Villa, our arms wrapped around each other, hurrying to get to our room, we almost bumped into a group of people in the vestibule. Rowena, Johnny and Luigi were talking excitedly to two people who had just arrived... my father and Lucinda Sackville-Jones.

33

'Pa, whatever are you doing here? And Lucinda?' I left Adam' side and embraced my father. He held me for a moment or two longer than our usual restrained hug, and I breathed in his familiar perfume. A discreet manly cologne, old-world style and a whiff of something indefinable. He had long given up smoking cigars, but it was a rich aroma... maybe even coffee, wool tweed or log fires? Comforting though. I glanced up at him, and he was looking at me with a frown as he replied,

'Now that's a fine greeting after I have suffered the indignity and discomfort of what I am told is a ticketless airline. Lucinda convinced me it was the quickest way to Ancona so here we are... travel worn and crumpled. You cannot imagine how wonderful it was to find Bernard waiting outside the airport.'

I turned to Bernard, 'So this is all your doing, is it? You knew about this but didn't say anything at breakfast?'

Bernard nodded and gave one of his stern smiles but made no reply and Lucinda spoke next,

'We've been so worried about you, Eve... and you, too, Adam. Ever since the media spread the story of your mugging and now this!' She waved her long arm in the general direction of the forest below the Villa. I studied her closely and decided she looked incredibly well. The dark shadows below her deep-set, almost violet eyes had completely disappeared.

Her cheeks were pink, and there was a trace of lipstick on her mouth. Yes, Lucinda had obviously recovered from her bout of alcoholism. I was just thinking that it was all due to Adam taking her under his wing when to my surprise, my father put his arm around Lucinda's tiny waist and hugged her to him. I almost squeaked with shock and immediately looked at Adam. His dark blonde eyebrows were raised in surprise as he caught my glance and then smiled as he said quickly,

'Why don't we all move on in. It seems we all have a lot to catch up on, Mr Sinclair...' Adam paused and looked at my father hesitantly, 'Sorry, I know you asked me to call you Robert, but it doesn't come easily yet. So, Robert, have you heard all about last night's adventure?'

'Indeed, I have. I'm not sure whether to tear you off a strip for leading my daughter into danger or thank you for saving her life.'

I saw the lump in Adam's throat move as he swallowed hard, 'Well, sir, I suppose I can only hope that one will cancel out the other?'

'Maybe so, maybe so. I have to agree with Bernard who has told me the whole story, including the fact that my daughter is a wilful creature and does exactly as she wants. My fault for spoiling her, of course.'

I was walking behind my father and Adam as they spoke about me. I had no time to feel resentful at their words, and the way they were treating me as a naughty child, as I was totally absorbed with watching my father's hand resting on Lucinda's skinny ribcage. Was he actually squeezing her thin body to him? My head was spinning, and my breath came in small gasps. Had I just become accustomed to sharing a little of Adam with Lucinda to find I had to begin again with my father? Well, it was no joke to say that he was old enough to be her father. Lucinda was exactly my age, after all, we had been in the same year at school. I tried to take a deep breath as I calculated ages, yes, my father had been just twenty-two when I was born. A young father starting out on his career and in love with his wayward beautiful wife. How wrong that had gone. I sighed and returned to my calculations. So there was an age difference of twenty-two years or so. It did seem a lot but, of course, I knew several of my father's friends had remarried young women. It was almost normal in the wealthy stressful life of business tycoons. But my father, surely not? My thoughts were interrupted by Bernard's quiet voice in my ear,

'I called your father, Mademoiselle Eve, *mais oui*. He has been so very anxious since he heard of the attack on you and Rowena. I had no idea until this morning that he intended to come here...' he hesitated and then added, 'avec Mademoiselle Lucinda. This I did not know at all, rien de tout.'

I murmured quietly back, 'Yes, well, it's certainly a surprise if not a shock. Don't worry Bernard. I suppose I should be used to my father always doing the unthinkable.'

As I spoke, we had all reached the small salon at the back of the Villa. We settled ourselves down on the comfortable chairs and sofas, and Adam suggested he would order drinks.

'Coffee anyone or...' he paused, aware that anything stronger might be a bad idea, 'or tea, perhaps?'

I looked at my father curiously, this was definitely the sort of occasion when he would order his favourite Champagne and make a fuss if Louis Roederer Crystal could not be supplied in good chilled quantity. To my surprise, he clapped his hands and said,

'Good idea, Adam, green tea for Lucinda and me, how about the rest of you?'

I felt the colour rush to my cheeks at his words. So, was I to be included in the 'rest of you' while he was bracketed with Lucinda. I began to feel the situation to be intolerable and was about to rise from my seat when Adam said,

'I'll find a member of staff on my way to the lift. Eve and I have been for a walk, so we need a wash and brush up. We'll join you all for lunch at one.'

Before anyone had time to object, especially my father who was already looking a little startled, Adam held out his hand to me. I grabbed it, and we almost ran from the room together.

By the time we reached the lift, we were both laughing helplessly. Whether it was delayed shock, tiredness or I know not what, but all my tense feelings of jealousy and anger vanished into the enclosed air of the lift. I leant against Adam laughing so much that I could hardly stand. As the lift door opened his swept me up in his arms and ran to our bedroom door, almost dropping me as he fumbled with the key. Once inside we fell on the bed together, and I managed to stop laughing enough to say,

'I can't believe it! My Pa with Lucinda Sackville-Jones? It's just not possible, is it?'

'Looks like it to me.' Adam rubbed the tears of laughter from his eyes, 'Who'd have thought it? The old Devil. Still, it's obvious really, you know, she wants a father figure, and he has just lost his one and only precious daughter to this disreputable but amazingly young and handsome photographer. It's Greek, isn't it? Oedipus or some ancient Greek geyser?'

'Oh, don't! You'll make me start laughing all over again. But I suppose you're right. Good luck to them both, I suppose.'

'Do you mean that, Princess? I mean, that's a very grown-up thing to say.'

'Is it? I don't know, somehow it doesn't seem that important. I have you and that's all that matters.'

'I love you, Eve. Sorry I keep calling you Princess. I know you hate it and think it's vulgar.'

'Hmm, well, I'm beginning to like it now, just sometimes when we're together.'

'Like now, Princess?'

'Oh yes, exactly like now when we're close together.'

I was beginning to feel that I didn't care about anything at all. Adam was very slowly unbuttoning my shirt, carefully removing the rosebud and holding it in his teeth. I stretched back on the bed, giving myself up to the ideas of the future, near and far. Adam broke into my dreams saying,

'You have broken your promise to me though...' he paused and ran his hand slowly between my breasts. 'You did promise to explain the rhyming pattern of that other Greek guy, Petrarch.'

I laughed and said, 'Why, so I did. I'd never break a promise I made to you, Adam, you know that.'

Then I began to unbutton his shirt and added, 'It's all about rhythm and pattern. The Petrarchan sonnet has three quatrains ABBA ABBA CDEC and then DE the closing couplet.

'Oh yes, I remember now, I think you told me that... I certainly remember the close coupling, oh yes...

EPILOGUE

    Adam and I sat side by side in the squashy white leather seats of a private jet.

    Adam placed his hand over mine on the wide armrest and asked,

    'Is this what you meant about your father taking things over?'

    I leant my head back into the soft curve of the head-rest and nodded,'

    'It's exactly what I meant.'

    'Well, it's not all bad.'

    'I know, it can be very comforting, and it's invariably luxuriously comfortable.'

    'Are you over being mad at him?'

    'Oh yes, completely. Well, I think so anyway. I've decided to accept the fact that he's liable to do unacceptable things.'

    'He does seem to have a good effect on Lucinda. She's so happy and relaxed.'

    'I know, maybe my father is just what she needs. Oedipal comfort, like sitting in white leather. She's so welcome.'

    'You mean that, don't you. You're so grown up, Princess.'

    'I think I must be. Bernard was so sweet when we said *au revoir*. He said he had never been more proud of me. I'm not sure why, but it was good to hear.'

'He said something similar to me, too. Something about feeling happy to leave me in charge of you.'

'Huh, in charge indeed. If I weren't so newly grown up, I'd resent that. As it is I shall just smile secretly.'

'Oh please don't! Give a proper Garbo smile, please, just one of those remote knowing ones. So sexy.'

'Behave yourself, Adam. It's no good flirting and thinking about sex on a private jet.'

'That's disappointing. I thought that's what it was all about. Haven't you heard of the Mile High Club?' Adam swung up the arm-rest between us and moved closer to me, slipping his hand into the opening of my shirt.

I elbowed him sharply in the ribs, even though I was breathing in the familiar, seductive aroma that wafted from him, 'I told you to behave. Now sit back quietly and play with your iPad.'

'Very disappointing,' Adam sighed. 'That was a sigh of frustration, in case you want to add it to our list. Just you wait until we get home, Princess Grown-up.'

'I can't wait either, I promise.'

'You do always keep your promises, too.'

'Of course, I do. I never promise anything I can't be sure I can do.'

'Then I'm happy to be in a private jet and the quickest possible way home.'

I was quiet for a moment, thinking about home and the meaning of the word. Such a dinky little word that conveyed so much feeling. Short and sweet, derived from the Old English hām, of course. Like house, the Old English hūs, both straightforward little words of Germanic origin. Adam broke into my thoughts,

'You're off in one of your Eve-reveries, aren't you? I know you are. A penny for your thoughts?'

'My thoughts are worth so much more, you know that, my love.' I paused, wondering whether to explain that I had slipped into a train of thought related to my love of words. I decided to take an easier path,

'I was thinking how good it will be to get back to our flat in London. Our home.'

'I know. The Villa was an extraordinary place to stay, but I do love our loft.' Then he turned to me, his blue eyes worried, 'Do you wish we were going back to your place in Provence?'

I thought about that for a moment. I loved it there, of course, and at this time of the year, as the summer rolled into Autumn, the air would be gentle, perfumed by wild herbs. How could I not wish to be there? But I said firmly,

'Oh well, we'll take a break there as soon as we can. I have to collate my work, and you have to get back for your exhibition and to check out the kids' workshop with Lucinda. Too much to do at the moment.' I stifled a sigh of regret and allowed the image in my mind of my beautiful Provencal *mas* to fade away.

Adam yawned and said. 'I suppose so. I am worried that Lucinda might let me down.'

'What do you mean?' Now I looked at Adam in concern.

'Well, supposing she flies off to India with your Dad?'

'Oh no, she talked to me about that. She told me she was dedicated to the young people at the workshop. She said my father is going to come back to London and just make visits to Kerala. Apparently, he has excellent managers at the tourist village now.'

'Really? Well, that is a relief. I thought it might be the other way round. I could quite imagine Luc turning your father into a long-haired hippy, smoking pot in a thatched hut in Kerala.'

I laughed out loud at the idea and pressed the overhead buzzer.

'Shall we order drinks? Orange juice?'

'Good idea. I noticed your father is supporting Luc by keeping off the booze. I remember at our wedding the Champagne ran like tap water. He's gone teetotal.'

'I know, but he never does anything in half measures. It will be good for him anyway. Better than smoking pot in a hut beside the Indian Ocean.' I laughed again at the thought and then added, 'We did a good thing this time, didn't we? Stopping the drug traffickers, I mean.'

'Yep, the Carabinieri were very pleased with us, even Bernard forgot to be cross with me. He said the Carabinieri had been checking all the excessive electric bills locally but, of course, there was a generator at that place. What a hell hole! That ghastly factory and then all that marijuana.'

'Marijuana? I didn't see that. What do you mean?'

'I suppose you were just behind me when that door rolled up.'

'I was blinded with the bright light...'

'Exactly. I saw inside for a second before I was tasered and knocked down. There was a bloomin' forest of marijuana plants, growing under huge overhead lights. You know, the sort they have over snooker tables.'

I struggled to imagine what he meant and then said, 'Oh, I know what you mean, those trapezium-shaped lights? We had two over our table in the billiard room in the house in Kensington.'

Adam laughed, 'We have so much in common, don't we, my love.'

We stayed silent for a minute or two, I think we were both playing back the scene of that dreadful night. Then, I said,

'Such a shock to find out it was Signor Marioni running the whole miserable business.'

'I had the sort of idea it could be him. I saw his watch when we were spying on the factory. It caught the light when he checked the time. Not many people wear a Rolex Submariner. Then, I remembered

Luigi telling us about his father's powerful yacht. It all added up.'

'Why didn't you tell me?'

'What, there in the middle of the yard? Anyway, minutes later we were both out cold. There was hardly a chance for a chat, was there?'

I nodded, 'Luigi took it very well, and by now he'll already be in rehab. I think Rowena handled the whole thing very well, leaving before we did.'

'She's a competent young woman. Quite able to keep Johnny and Luigi under her wing and in good order. Her baby will have a fine mother. One lucky kiddo.'

I nodded again, 'I would have liked to leave with them, but I had to sort out my work.'

'I know, I dreaded you were going to say that you'd have to find another Verdicchio, start all over again for the chapter. But, thank the Gods, you pulled it out of the hat. I have so many outstanding photos, too.'

'Outstanding? You do like to praise yourself, don't you?'

'Well, I have to, no-one else cares.'

'Apart from your collection of awards, I suppose. Photographer of the year, wasn't it?'

'That's all very well, but I need constant approval. I'm very insecure and needy, you know.'

I burst out laughing at the sad face he was pulling and ruffled his hair as I said, 'You look just like Butterscotch. Really, Adam, you are a clown. But seriously, I was determined not to give up on my choice of Verdicchio. I know you suggested the wines from the Leopardi estate, but I wasn't happy with the idea. I always want my signature to be on the label of a truly excellent and unusual wine. I know the Leopardi wines, they have a good selection, not just Verdicchio but other Marchigiani wines from the Conero and … in fact, a quite good red Conero…' I shook my head and said, 'But I don't want you nodding off to sleep so I won't tell you all about the others on their list. Anyway, Signora Marioni was so helpful and knew so much. I have loads of information now.'

'What a woman! Really gutsy American with a great love for Italy and tradition. And how Butterscotch took to her straight away. That was a good idea of Luigi's.' Adam paused then added, 'But I shall miss Butterscotch. I wish we could have taken him home with us.'

'Don't be ridiculous, Adam. How could we possibly keep a Rottweiler in our loft in Clerkenwell?'

'I know. I know but...'

I interrupted him sharply, 'Anyway, Butterscotch will be an excellent guard dog at Casa Verde.'

'Hmm, not so sure about that. Butterscotch has more the mentality of a lapdog.'

'Well, at least he looks the part. Anyway, You're just being selfish. The dog will be much happier living in the beautiful Marchigiana countryside.

'I know you're right, but you can't stop me missing him.' Adam stretched his hands above his head and said, 'Do you think it was true that Signor Marioni knew nothing of her husband's drug smuggling? It was impressive how very calm and collected she remained when the Carabinieri interviewed her.'

'Cool, as Luigi would say.' We both laughed at the thought, and I added, 'I'm just relieved that she was found innocent. I could hardly write about a vineyard owned by a drug runner. No, it all worked out well. I liked her and believed her, on the whole.' I thought about it all for a moment and then said, 'I've invited her to come to London soon. I said I'd introduce her to Melanie and show her around a bit. Maybe it will take her mind off worrying about Luigi.'

'That's a kind thought, Princess, a very grown-up idea. She could visit the workshop, maybe pose for a portrait session. The kids love meeting people from different backgrounds. Not sure if you should let Melanie loose on the poor woman though.'

'On the contrary, I'm going to persuade Melanie to take on the Casa Verde as a client. She can use some of your outstanding photos on a new website.'

'Can she indeed? My, you're quite the Princess Fixer, aren't you?'

'Yes, I suppose I am. I think that just about wraps everything up for this assignment. Soon we must start planning our next trip to Bardolino.'

'Is it a very nice quiet place on a beautiful lake in Italy?'

'Indeed, it is.'

'Can we try and keep it that way? Do you promise there won't be trouble afoot, Princess?'

'I never make promises I can't keep, Adam, you know that.'

THE END

WINE DARK MYSTERIES

Well Chilled   Case 1: Haute Savoie to Provence
Skin Contact   Case 2: Provence
Lingering Finish   Case 3: Roussilon
Rich Earthy Tuscany   Case 4: Chianti
Mistaken Identities   Case 5: Frascati, Rome
Fine Racy Wine   Case 6: Newmarket, Suffolk
Horizontal Tasting   Case 7 Loire Valley
Full Bodied Lush   Case 8: Gascony
Pink Fizz   Case 9   Kent

and romantic thrillers

Perfume of Provence
Provence Love Legacy
Provence Flame
Provencal Landscape of Love
Provence Starlight
Provence Snow
Dreams of Tuscany
Moonlight in Tuscany
Love on an Italian Lake

and a longer book by Kate's clever sister,
EVA FITZROY
Long Shadow of Love

Printed in Great Britain
by Amazon